HABITS AND LOVE

A segment of the title story "Habits and Love" appeared in the anthology *2000% Cracked Wheat*, Coteau Press, 1999.

"A Good Man" appeared in *Wascana Review*, August, 1997.

"The Vast and Greatly Huge" appeared in *The Fiddlehead*, Summer, 1997.

"Driving Home" appeared in *Pottersfield Portfolio*, May, 1996.

Habits and Love

Short Stories

by

Rod Schumacher

INSOMNIAC PRESS

Edited by Jan Barbieri
Copy Edited by Richard Almonte
Designed by Jonathan Blackburn

National Library of Canada Cataloguing in Publication Data

Schumacher, Rodney Donald, 1951-
  Habits and Love

ISBN 1-894663-16-0

I. Title

PS8587.C564H32 2002 C813'.6 C2002-900746-1
PR9199.4.S38H32 2002

The publisher gratefully acknowledges the support of the Canada Council, the Ontario Arts Council and Department of Canadian Heritage through the Book Publishing Industry Development Program.

The author gratefully acknowledges the financial support of the Canada Council during the completion of this book.

Printed and bound in Canada

Insomniac Press
192 Spadina Ave., Suite 403,
Toronto, ON, Canada, M5T 2C2
www.insomniacpress.com

THE CANADA COUNCIL | LE CONSEIL DES ARTS
FOR THE ARTS | DU CANADA
SINCE 1957 | DEPUIS 1957

ONTARIO ARTS COUNCIL
CONSEIL DES ARTS DE L'ONTARIO

for JLS

TABLE OF CONTENTS

THIS GUY AT THE LAUNDROMAT

One day Jake and me are killing time in the laundromat at the Avalon Plaza. It has already stopped raining, but we're still sitting around, not doing much, just shooting the shit. We've already checked the machines and payphone for change, and rifled through the lost and found looking for women's underwear, but there's nothing worth getting excited about.

Then the door slices open and this guy strides in with a load of clothes and looking like he just ate a fistful of nasty-pills. He's one of those crewcut types, so I figure he's either in the army or just out of prison. A tidy blonde carrying a baby comes in behind him. The guy goes to the rear of the building, drops the basket on the counter, then heads back to the door. Jake and me are parked on the bench by the door and when we see him look at us we both put our heads down and start studying the lino real seriously. It's no use though, because before you could say jack-spit these shiny black shoes are in front of us. Now I figure the guy is definitely army—no criminal would wear shoes like that. I also figure being in the army is the worst of the two possibilities because not only does it prove he's crazy, it also means he knows how to kill.

Then this voice booms down, "What are you two doing in here?"

Jake and me sneak a sideways look at each other. We don't say nothing, but I know we're both wondering if two fourteen year olds can do any passable shit-kicking. Jake's face tells me we're both gonna die.

He says, "You kids make that mess in here last week? Sprayed pop all over the walls?"

Jake starts to shuffle his feet, like he's going to make a break for it, so I look up and give the guy my best I-don't-know-what-you're-talking-about look. But I guess it doesn't work because the next thing I know he has me by the shoulders and is shoving me to the door.

"Hey!" I yell. "What gives you the right to kick us out?"

He uses my face to open the door, then says, "This is my right," and buries his shoe in my butt. I hit the sidewalk on all fours then spin around just in time to see Jake fake him once to the left then deke under his arm. The guy swings a fist at the back of his head but Jake is already past him and on the sidewalk. As the door closes, he looks at me, this big Alfred E. Newman smile on his face, like he just cleaned up the wild west.

A group of guys stop checking out the barber's new car and walk over to see what's going on. Pretty soon there's about ten of us standing in the parking lot and Jake is busy giving everyone the lowdown and showing them the move he put on the guy. When he's finished we all start talking about getting back at the guy. After all, he doesn't own the place, so why should he care about a little pop on the walls? They can see I'm pretty steamed up so I figure I've got to do something, but I don't know what. The other guys, they've got lots of ideas because they don't have to do anything. Everybody's busy inventing tortures and laughing hard at the best ones, and the whole time the guy keeps watching and pacing back and forth inside the laundromat. The gang goes wild when Jake says we should drag him to the edge of town, strip him buck-naked and shove barbed wire up his ass. When he starts pretending like he's sticking it to the guy they all put their hands over their butts, screw up their faces and start hopping on their tiptoes, dancing around crazy, like they just moved down from living in the trees. Then a cop car pulls up beside us.

As soon as the cop gets out the guy and the blonde head straight for the baby-blue Hyundai Pony parked out front. Everybody starts groaning about the guy being a chickenshit because he phoned the cops and because after all the waiting nothing happened. As the Pony putts away the guy sticks his arm out the window, points a finger at my head, and mouths *POW,* then throws in another smile. The cop just stands there watching the whole thing. Then he asks us what's going on. I fill him in on the whole business. He listens, nods and smiles a bit when he sees how pissed off I am. I ask him what would've happened if I'd kicked the guy back; I'm thinking about legal stuff— getting arrested, lawyers, court, assault. All the cop says is that I would've been in over my head and something about Bambi and Godzilla. The cop's all right. He hangs around and shoots the bull with us. Everyone wants to know about his cruiser. How big is the motor? What's the horsepower? How fast can it go? Asking about all the gear and crap screwed to the dash. After five minutes of getting grilled he takes off.

We hang around for a bit, talking back and forth about what it'd be like to be a cop and what a peckerhead the guy in the Pony was. Pretty soon we break up and me and Jake wander over to the school grounds to see if anything's going on over there.

A few weeks later we come out of the Tastee Freeze — me starting in on a monster-size Swamp-Water Float, and Jake staggering and squeezing his head with both hands and hollering, "Brain freeze! Brain freeze!" because he chugged a Coke too fast. But he settles right down when we spot the blue Hyundai in front of the laundry. Then he tells me to stay put while he checks it out. I wait at the corner, watching as he makes a quick pass in front of the laundry window, looks inside, then gives me the thumbs-up sign. Then he takes off to let the guys near the bakery know what's going on.

I slip behind the barber's car and squat out of sight. In no time at all I hear them gathering over by the bakery. They're already laughing and someone's passing around a bag of doughnuts. While I'm waiting I notice the paint on the bottom of the barber's car has already started to chip. I'm thinking it's a real shame, considering he's only had it a couple of months, when I hear the laundromat door open. I set my float beside the tire and get down on my hands and knees, and watch as two shiny black shoes step off the sidewalk and stop beside the Pony. The guy's back is toward me so I get up slowly and look over the trunk. He's holding his laundry and checking out the gang from the bakery. As I slip up behind him Jake starts throwing some lip at the guy to keep him distracted. Just as I'm about to let him have it I spot the blonde standing just inside the laundromat. She's looking right at me, rocking the baby in her arms, her face blank like she's in shock or something. I figure I better get the guy quick before she comes to, so I wind up and sink my foot as hard as I can right up his crack.

By the time he turns around the gang at the bakery are ki-yiing like crazy and I'm making dust. Jake bellows out one of his twisted one-liners, "You're a bigger Gunga Din than me, man!" and I can hear the guy start after me, swearing to beat all. I put my head down and just keep on pumping. At the end of the plaza I take a quick look back. There's no way he's going to catch me. I ease up and keep an eye on him as I cross the street. He's still coming on, though, but when he reaches the edge of the parking lot he's puffing so hard he knows he has no chance and stops. We exchange a few basic comments across the pavement. He finishes by saying he won't forget my face. I tell him he better watch it because I know where he lives. I don't know why I say it, it's not true, but it sure surprises the hell out of him.

Then it's my turn to shoot him in the head, but I don't mouth *POW*. That really pisses him off, but all he does is shake a fist at me before heading back to his car. I follow at a distance.

All the guys give him lots of room as he goes by. When I join them they all start whacking me on the back, punching my shoulders, hooting. The blonde is finished picking up the laundry from the pavement and she's sitting in the car staring straight ahead. Mr. Crewcut takes a final look at us, his face red, the veins in his neck about to pop. Then he gets in the car and slams the door. We move out into the parking lot as he guns the engine. The tires spin when he pulls out, then a little chirp as they grab the pavement. Everyone is still whacking me and laughing. Jake hands me my Swamp-Water, but it's all gone. Then he crouches down and starts into his impression of me sneaking up behind guy.

As the car reaches the edge of the lot I see the guy's arm flash into the air and the woman's head snap back. It happens so fast. I look at the guys around me but none one of them seem to have seen it. They're busy watching Jake. They're all still laughing.

A GOOD MAN

As the day wore on she knew there was no use trying to salvage the last leg of the holiday—it would likely be days before they'd even begin to acknowledge each other. Clank's head, cocked toward the side window, appeared to be trying to escape from his body as he leaned over the steering wheel. The cab was filled with a stubborn silence.

He knew he had already pushed the pickup down the gravel road several hours longer than Jane had wanted. He glanced at the clock on the dash—another hour and tomorrow they'd be within shooting distance of home. Jane sat, staring blankly at the blur of trees beside the road, her arms crossed over her chest.

"Clank," she said, the words coming from somewhere deep inside her body, "I want to stop for the night."

She waited a moment, then rolled her head away from the window to face him. The corner of his mouth twitched, but he refused to show any sign of having heard her.

More words began to gather inside her—there was a stirring in her stomach like goldfish bumping their noses against the glass, searching for a way out. For the past day he had walled himself off from the rest of the family; and as far as Jane was concerned, he may as well not even be there. Drive and smoke, drive and smoke, that's all he'd done since Vancouver.

"Look at the boys." Her head gestured sharply to the back of the cab. "They're going to get stiff necks sleeping like that."

Clank looked in the rear-view mirror at the two boys crowded into the tiny side-seats.

"They're kids," he said, his eyes already back on the road. "They can sleep anywhere. They don't care."

"Well, I'm not a kid and I'm sick of driving. Sick of this damn road, going who knows where." She knew it was useless. Trying to rant or reason—hell, trying to communicate anything when he was like this was a waste of time. But she'd had enough of his utter lack of concern for anyone else, this silent high ground he used against her. "Just because you're driving doesn't give you the right to do what you want."

"What I want is to get this ridiculous holiday over with so I can go back to work for another fifty goddamn weeks and get some peace and quiet."

The lights of an oncoming vehicle came into view. Even in the receding light it was easy to see the huge trail of grey dust billowing behind it.

"Damn it!" he said, his hands mechanically closing windows and vents. He had shut off the air in the cab so many times during the day that he no longer had to look at what he was doing. Jane left her window open, waiting until the last moment to seal herself in again.

As soon as they had left Vancouver the weather had turned unbearably hot, and as they drove further away from the coast the whole province seemed to dry up in front of them. Earlier, Clank had nearly put the truck in the ditch when she said they should have taken the Trans-Canada instead of the shortcut through Lillooet that a buddy at the mill had told him about. Even when she had complained she knew it was too late to turn back—it would have taken them until midnight just to get back to Vancouver. But she had wanted to bait him, get him mad enough that he would say something, anything. He had gone a bit crazy for a second, grabbing the top of the steering wheel with both hands, jerking his upper body around to face her, causing the truck to fishtail on the gravel. She was certain they were all going to die out there in the middle of bloody nowhere. She had kept quiet after that, but now her brain was beginning to beat against her skull. She took a deep breath then rolled up the window as the truck plowed into a wall of dust.

Clank's mood had gone from bad to worse since the truck had blown its radiator two days earlier. They were on a limited budget and the motel and repairs had put a serious dent in their funds. At first, he'd taken the setback in stride. He figured all he'd have to do is get a radiator from a wrecker in Hope or Chilliwack and put it in himself. There was a lake near the highway and he actually liked the idea of spending half a day under the truck while Jane and the boys enjoyed the beach. The weather was nice and everybody would have something to do. That was before he discovered he'd left his tools in the garage. He could see them sitting exactly where he had placed them on the end of the bench: everything in its place, the two metal boxes wiped clean and ready to be put in the camper. It was all that confusion before leaving—the boys constantly dragging stuff in and out of the camper, Jane yelling directions at everyone through the kitchen window while she talked to her mom on the phone about watering the plants and checking the mail. It was nothing at all like a clean getaway. One hundred and fifty dollars to install a radiator wasn't exactly highway robbery—they'd been lucky there—but he couldn't stop festering over paying someone to do a job he could have easily done himself. Every little thing that happened from that point on held a weight he was less and less willing to carry: the boys fighting over toys; trying to find their way around Vancouver; even the forced smile on Jane's face as she pointed out the teenagers with purple or orange hair, bag-ladies and totem poles. And then later, after finally escaping the city, having to suffer through the heat and dust, all of them trapped in this tin box on wheels. It all settled around him, on him, contained him. Was there any way to shed all this weight, even for just a day, an hour? And where would he go?

Just after ten o'clock, Clank finally gave in and pulled into a small clearing in the bush. They both climbed out of the cab in silence and stood for a moment, facing the darkness, each of them grateful for the truck that separated them. Jane wanted to talk it out, test the waters with a seemingly throwaway comment about the heat finally being gone. But the day had taken too much out of her, and whatever was passing between them was not to be trusted. She knew her words would be chosen out of exhaustion and would be too dangerous—sparks landing near a fuse. Clank made the first move as he gathered up one of the boys from the back seat and carried him into the camper. Jane thought to pull the sleeping bags from the two beds and shake off the dust, but the effort struck her as an extravagant waste of energy. After getting the boys settled and opening all the windows, they dropped their sweaty clothes on the floor and collapsed onto the bed.

Sometime later Clank was awakened by the sound of a vehicle and headlights streaking across the inside of the camper. *More happy campers*, he thought to himself as he rolled over and fell back to sleep.

Then he was awake again, wide awake. A confusing din filled the camper. A red flickering in the windows. He sat up in a panic, sniffing the air. *Forest fire!* he thought. *Right outside the camper!* He was out of bed and heading to the door when he realized what the noise was. Fear turned to rage as his mind registered the raucous laughter and music.

Jane raised her head. "What's going on?"

Clank was at the door. "Nothing much," was his matter-of-fact reply.

She saw his arm reach into the corner. Then the door flew open and whacked against the outside wall. She heard glass breaking. For just a second she saw him clearly: his tall, bony frame bending through the doorway, the boxer shorts with "Come And Get It" printed all over them in bright colours, the boys' baseball bat clenched in his right hand. Then he plunged out the door like a paratrooper.

"Clank?" she cried, her voice tight and thin from dust and fear. But he was gone.

Fifty feet from the truck four figures were sitting around a fire. A portable tape deck, belting out music, sat on a stump at the edge of the circle. Clank walked straight toward the fire.

He pierced the campfire's red-yellow light so abruptly that the first person to see him, a woman in her early twenties, screamed and fell off the log she was sitting on. The three others, two men and another woman of the same age, were also caught off guard but managed to remain seated. They looked up, stupefied by the wild, half-naked apparition that had suddenly flared into their world.

Clank stood over them, his lank body glowing in the light. His eyes glared from face to face then settled on the tape deck. As if on cue, their eyes turned to the bat. As the tape deck pounded chaos into the night, Clank raised the bat slowly over his head, held it there for a moment, then brought it down with a thundering crash. Shards of plastic and metal exploded into the darkness. A deep silence seemed to drop from the sky.

For a moment the four sat staring in disbelief at the shattered tape deck. Then one of the young men—thick-skinned, stocky, a crude beard covering his cheeks and neck—raised his head and stared defiantly at Clank. Even if there hadn't been a half-dozen beer cans spread on the ground, Clank would have known that this fellow sizing him up was well into a night of heavy drinking. Clank had stuck his face into enough late nights in the past to recognize this scene. It had been a long time, but he was quick to feel the warmth of adrenaline rush through his veins.

The eyes of the younger man had no depth. They were clouded and rolled from side to side, reminding Clank of a Magic-8-Ball with a window that tells the future on a floating lump inside. Clank's eyes had nothing of the future in them. It didn't bother him that he was outnumbered by two men fifteen years younger than himself. He liked the idea of being the underdog. He glanced at the other fellow and made a quick tally: same age as his buddy, not as drunk, clean shaven, thinner, likely faster, some nervous hand movements. Sure, he might get smacked around, maybe lose some teeth, but that would be nothing compared to what he would do to them. Clank had one thing on his mind: he wanted to inflict pain, give these two bozos something to remember him by. Winning was nothing; damage was what really counted.

He dragged the bat across the log, squinted and growled one word: "Go!"

The girls started to their feet, as did the thinner man, but the stocky one across the fire refused to budge.

"Come on, Bill," said one of the girls. "Let's get out of here."

The man rose cautiously, testing his legs, trying not to give away his imbalanced state. His eyes darted to the left, then to the right, searching for something to match the bat. The three friends stepped back and stood behind Bill. The other man leaned over and whispered something to his friend. Bill nodded in agreement.

Once again the same girl spoke out, in a sharper voice, "Come on, let's split. No big deal." She bent down and tugged at the shoulder of his shirt.

Bill seemed to rise a bit above his drunken macho stance, his eyes gaining a hint of sharpness, but not because of what the girl had said. He had seen movement in the dark, directly behind Clank. A figure emerged: a woman dressed in an oversized plaid shirt, her arms waving, the palms of her hands pushing at the air in front of her, signalling him to be quiet, telling him to go away.

Jane knew what Clank was capable of doing when he got like this. She had left him once, six years ago, because of his wildness. Originally she had been attracted by his sudden outbursts, the threat of danger that surrounded him, how he thrived in precarious environments. She shivered remembering how he would leap forward and stand up to anyone with a nose for trouble. His world had been new to her—there was always some element of risk involved in being near him. But she quickly learned there was no place she couldn't go with him where she didn't feel secure; even the way he walked made the roughest looking people stand aside. He was more at ease in a crowd of bikers than eating at McDonald's. But when she found out she was pregnant her mind became very clear: if they were going to stay together, Clank would have to change.

And he did. He became more consistent, more responsible. He took a job at the mill. They began to spend most weekends at home, by themselves. He had agreed to buy some furniture from a real furniture store instead of secondhand junk from the classifieds. And then last year, they moved into their own house. But an edginess remained in him; a resentful moodiness would surface at times. If they were shopping, his step would become quicker, overly deliberate, as if he was trying to distance himself from her and the boys, and everything had to be done in half the expected time. She blamed it on the long hours and shift work at the mill, or on the supervisor who seemed to make it his goal to always get on Clank's case. When he was in one of his moods he would go through his silent routine and start doing mundane jobs like cleaning the garage, polishing his tools—anything that kept him out of the house. The surest sign of danger was when he began to cram whatever he had to say into one syllable words like "yeah," "no," "bed," and in this case, "Go!" When the timing was right, he could handle just about anything. When it was wrong, like now, his past could come rushing forward like a guard dog charging a fence. She didn't want to lose him, not now, not after they'd come so far. And who was this stranger across the fire? A kid really. And probably just as fearless and stupid as Clank was at that age. She clasped her hands in front of her chest and silently begged the young man to leave. In some way she wanted to mother him, warn him, make him come to his senses.

Clank noted the change in the young man, how his eyes appeared more focused, more cautious. He wanted to say something to get him going again. It wouldn't take much—call him a bush-bunny—and bingo, he'd be right back.

"Go!" he repeated. But this time the word seemed to have lost some of its former power. It sounded more like Clank was giving him permission to leave.

Bill's buddy stepped up, grabbed his arm and spoke in a half-whisper. "Come on man, this guy's crazy."

Bill wrenched his arm away, lost his balance and staggered sideways. When he recovered he seemed to realize his reflexes were worse than he'd hoped.

"Bill! We're leaving right now!" And then all three of them came forward and grabbed his arms and started pulling him to the car.

Clank had a pretty good idea what would happen next, and as he followed them to the car he couldn't help smiling as Bill began to wrestle and swing his fists at his friend. Bill put up just enough of a fight to make it look like he was unwilling to leave, but not enough to stop himself from being dragged away. Whenever he broke free he'd take a few wobbly steps toward the fire before being cut off, at which point he would start cursing his friend and his fists would fly through the air again.

Jane stepped back toward the camper. *Men*, she thought. *Why can't they see the outcome before they even get started? Why do they always have to get in over their heads?* In the end, there was either disaster or someone had to step in so they could save face. At the back of the truck she turned and looked at Clank, standing on the far side of the fire, his back facing her as he watched the four strangers get in their car. She wondered what would have happened if she'd been alone, or with a different kind of man, someone less likely to stand up to these people. What would that man have done? Would he have simply gotten up, started the truck and continued down the road? Would he have risked saying anything to them? Asked them to turn down the music or find another place to party? Would she have felt as safe? She thought not. Maybe those kids didn't intend any harm, but then again, they didn't intend to do any good either. And that Bill fellow, a real loose screw, she knew that much, and who knows what he might have done? No. She easily chose Clank over Mr. Mellow.

She brushed the glass from the step and climbed into the camper. The boys had slept through the whole ordeal. She sat on the bed and looked down at them. She couldn't help but hope that they would have at least some portion of Clank's sense of self-power. It would be better for them to be too confident, too self-assured. At least they'd be able to stand up for themselves, for their families.

She heard the car start, and then there were shouts and swearing, Bill's voice being the loudest, the most vulgar. Then the sound of spinning tires and gravel spraying like buckshot into the brush. As they reached the road one of the kids leaned onto the horn and held it down, as if getting in the last word. She lay on the bed listening to the blaring horn for what seemed an impossible length of time until it finally vanished.

Clank remained standing near the fire, watching the headlights cut through the trees until they finally disappeared around a corner. He felt light and smooth. As he turned back to the camper he became aware of the bat, still clenched in his hand. Clank looked down at the bat. His first thought was of his oldest son, his face bursting with amazement as he unwrapped it on his last birthday. He saw the boy reaching into the box, his toothless smile filling the room. Clank's stomach twisted. He knew he would never be able to look at the bat again, not this one. He took three deliberate steps, pitched himself forward and flung the bat into the black bushes.

From the bed, Jane could hear him rummaging in the storage compartment outside the door of the camper; then, further away, the hiss of water being poured on the fire. When he entered the camper he moved like a man who'd given up on himself.

"You all right honey?"

"Yeah," he replied.

"Do you think they'll come back?"

Clank crawled in beside her, dropped face-down on the bed and mumbled, "No," into the sleeping bag. His body lay heavy and motionless.

She turned on her side and began to rub his back—a slow rhythm, a gentle touch. After a few minutes he turned and faced her, his eyes looking into hers, then shifting to the darkness over her head. They lay in silence for a long time, their noses almost touching, sharing each other's breath, her hand still moving across his skin. His eyes finally settled on her. She gazed intently, almost forcefully at him, into him. He could feel her penetrating his consciousness.

"Clank?" her voice was clear and deliberately measured. "You are a good man."

His lips squeezed together as though he had to consider if there was any truth in what she said. A puff of air escaped through his nose—a gesture of disbelief. He rolled onto his back, his arm folding around her as she snuggled beside him. They stayed that way, quietly letting the night gather around them.

He stared at the ceiling, listening to her breathing become deeper and slower. His mind struggled in little circles of confusion, doubt, fear; each circle leading into the other, then beginning again with no resolution, no final answer. There was goodness in his life: Jane, the boys, a job, a house. And he wanted them all. But why was it so hard to keep it all intact, so hard to stay on top of everything? And where did he fit in? He could see the whole scene clearly, as if that very moment contained everything he had become: the camper sitting in a small clearing, surrounded by darkness and brush; the empty road winding through the dark; the whole valley nothing more than a rut in the earth. He could see it all. But how could he go about turning it into a life?

He strained to hear something, anything, but all he could hear was the blood pulsing through his ears. The harder he tried to listen past the sound in his head, the louder it became. And then in the distance, somewhere over the hills, the sound of thunder came rolling through the dry air toward him. He lay listening, waiting—knowing he had somehow stumbled into the eye of the storm, that tiny patch of calm where love is not a struggle.

DRIVING HOME

When Janet was nine it seemed like the whole country was tap dancing. Jack had signed her up for lessons, and in the evenings he would lay a piece of plywood on the kitchen floor and she would practice patterns in her shiny black shoes while he did a soft-shoe imitation beside her. Bonnie would watch from her chair by the table, nodding, offering a mother's dutiful encouragement and clapping at the end of the routines. It was clear to her that Janet was too clumsy and stiff to ever get close to a real stage. But Jack told her she was terrific. Back then he had a knack for telling everyone exactly what they needed to hear.

She can tell he doesn't want to talk by the way he pretends to be so absorbed in driving—checking the mirror and gauges every thirty seconds, eyes straining to see beyond the next curve. She knows he wants to control something, even if it's only a car.

"She'll be twenty-one in January," she says quietly, almost to herself. The words aren't directed at Jack—neither of them has said anything for the last ten miles—they're simply spoken and left to hang in the air or drop to the floor. Jack could say something if he wanted to, if he even heard her—she wouldn't mind that at all—but she knows he won't. It's a shared and agreed upon silence, an enduring silence, and light on the usual endearments one might expect after having lived together for over twenty-five years. Bonnie glances to her left; she can't tell if Jack's thinking about anything or trying to avoid thinking altogether. He's rolled his window down a few inches, just enough to suck some noise into the car so the silence isn't too obvious. She knows he doesn't want to hear what she's thinking.

They're on their way home from Janet's, their only child. She moved out a month ago and now lives forty miles down the valley in Vernon. They were invited for supper so Janet could show them her new home, at least that's what Bonnie had thought at the time. It was bad enough that Janet thought living in a cramped four-room suite in a stranger's basement was something to be proud of, but that was only the beginning. Bonnie knew there was another reason they had been invited when Janet met them at the door, overly jovial and nervous. She heard the sound of a bowl being put down in the kitchen followed by footsteps coming down the hall. She knew it was only a matter of time until it happened, but she could tell that Jack, too, felt like they had been ambushed. He looked respectable enough, she guessed, even handsome, now that she thought about it. "Hi, I'm Paul," he announced, extending his hand, a tea-towel draped casually over his shoulder, looking as if the two of them had been together for years. His grasp was firm and certain, and he smiled like he was practising to be a life-insurance salesman. She remembered thinking that at least Janet had the good sense to pick someone who had manners.

Later, when they were left alone for a minute, Jack had turned to her and said, "Hi, I'm Paul and I'm sleeping with your daughter." Bonnie wasn't shocked, though, and from what she could tell neither was Jack. Disappointed, yes, but not shocked. The word "shock" seemed to belong to some earlier era. In retrospect she believed she had held up fairly well, all things considered; she had even managed a smile when he first entered the room.

It's a muggy night, the air so thick it's an effort for her just to breathe. The traffic is light now that all the commuters have cleared off the highway. Jack is obviously in one of his slow modes, driving well below the limit, in no hurry to get this little trip over, so she settles in.

It should still be light outside, but the sky is heavy with dark clouds, and a hard wind keeps rocking the car, threatening to send it into a ditch. The month, the time of day, the heat and wind—it's all too familiar to her, as though they're driving into the past. She runs the figures through her head, just as she does every year at this time, quickly realizing Leah would be eleven now, the same age Janet was when Leah was born. She wonders if there's some significance in that. They hadn't planned on another child. Leah just came, like a tulip in winter, as though she willed herself into her short life. She's tempted to say something to Jack, something about both girls being eleven. Not so much because he'll have anything to say—he hasn't spoken Leah's name in years—but sometimes she needs to hear Leah's name, speak it out loud where it sounds real, where she can try to make sense of what she thinks. Bonnie was twenty-seven when Janet was born; thirty-eight for Leah. Too old, some said.

A few drops of rain hit the windshield and she wishes Jack would turn on the wipers. Instead, he lays his forearms on the wheel and leans forward, as if he's grateful for the added distraction. He still looks younger than he really is—aging gracefully, as Bonnie often says. But right now it seems like years since she's seen him smile, really smile, not at a joke or something in a movie, but like he used to when they first met, or when she was pregnant with Leah. A regular ambassador of joy, that's what he was back then. At the hospital even the doctor was caught up in his enthusiasm and let him help in the delivery. She can still see him standing at the end of the delivery bed with the mask over his face, the funny little cap tied to his head, staring wide-eyed between her legs. But everything wasn't right with little Leah. She didn't cry right away, and the next thing Bonnie knew, the doctor had sent her down the hall to be checked. They had hoped to go home right after the birth, that was Jack's idea. He wanted to look after both of them himself, Janet, too; but they had to stay. The doctors were worried because Leah's reflexes were poor and she wasn't eager to nurse.

Bonnie and Jack pretty well lived in the hospital for the next ten days. And then Jack said the doctors had done enough poking and needling, and it was time to take Leah home where she belonged. When he went to tell the nurses what they were going to do, two doctors appeared out of nowhere and tried to change his mind. Bonnie remembers watching him through the large window in the nursery, where she sat with Leah. She could easily hear Jack's voice rising through the glass as he demanded to know what was wrong with his baby. They said they weren't sure, and Jack said if they weren't sure what she had, then he wasn't sure she had anything. He had made a big scene and pressed them to give a name to Leah's problem. "Just give me a name," he had said. "If she's sick, then tell me what she's got!" Even to Bonnie it had sounded more like a diagnosis of last resort when one of the doctors said Leah had something called "a failure to thrive." Jack just laughed in the doctor's face. "That's not a disease," he shot back, "that's the general state of this hospital. Nobody thrives here."

Bonnie's body rocks forward, pressing into the seatbelt. She looks up and realizes Jack has taken his foot off the gas and is edging the car toward the side of the road. It's raining more now, and she is a bit surprised to see Jack has turned on the wipers without her noticing. A pickup passes and he shakes his head. Bonnie looks out the windshield just as the pickup jerks back into its lane, almost sending an oncoming car into a ditch. "Kids," she says. "Damn kids." Jack is still shaking his head, but not in anger. It's as if he's too tired to even bother complaining.

If only Leah had gained some weight after Jack brought them home. She remembers someone saying that certain babies don't realize they are physical beings, that they're still attached to the spiritual world they came from and haven't made the bond with their bodies. Bonnie still thinks there is some kind of truth in that; it was as though her body wouldn't wake up. Yet Leah looked so beautiful, so perfect. And Jack, well, he simply marvelled over her hands, her feet, how her nails were so elegant, so—and Bonnie stops for a moment, wanting to recall the exact word he used—civilized, yes, that's what he said. And though she was wasting away in front of them, she was unbelievably content; she never made so much as a peep. How many times had Bonnie rubbed her nipple against Leah's soft lips to try to get her to suck? When she wouldn't respond Bonnie would open her tiny mouth and place a nipple between her lips. And Leah would just lie there, passive, no sign of hunger, no desire. She slept all the time. Bonnie had pinched her at times, secretly. She was gentle at first, going so far as to pretend to herself that it was nothing more than a game any mother with a normal healthy baby would play; then later, hard enough to leave little white marks on her flesh. She had felt sick and desperate doing it, and just plain disgusted with herself ever since.

She pulls herself up in the seat and rubs her hands briskly over her cheeks, as if to wipe away every thought. But it's all piling up in her, a monstrous force that refuses to be held back any longer.

And twice, yes, not once but twice, she had left nail marks, deep little creases that looked like Leah had been bitten by rats. And once, just once, it was all she could do to stop herself from trying to shake and slap and heave that perfect body into the world she was meant to belong in.

The doctors had kept calling, saying they needed to do more tests, then going so far as to threaten them with a court order. Finally, after two weeks, Jack agreed to admit her back into the hospital. They put her in a Plexiglass box, stuck wires on her chest, an I.V. in her tiny arm. Then the x-rays, blood and stool samples, and a thousand other procedures that Bonnie couldn't even pronounce. The doctors had spoken of cystic fibrosis, nerve connections in her brain, but they weren't sure, they were never sure of anything. Jack couldn't bear to see her lying alone in that box with all those wires. He had kept saying Leah needed to be held, that she had to feel people touching her and that if she could sense how much they loved her, she would want to live. Time and again Bonnie had come back to the hospital after going home to change or eat or nap, knowing for certain that Jack had spent hours on end kneeling on the floor, his arm inserted through one of the holes in the side of the box, his hand stuffed into a latex glove, gently stroking her skin while he whispered and sang to her.

In the end Bonnie had been the one who screamed at the doctors, at God; and both of them tried to believe there was some divine purpose in it all. They had talked, tried to say everything to each other—how much she meant to them, how important the few little sounds she made were—both of them wanting to believe there were some magic words that would lessen the hurt, carry it away like husks in the wind. They talked until they arrived at a point where all they could do was repeat the same words, the same gestures. It was as if they had reached so far into themselves that they hit some kind of bottom—a place where silence grows like moss in a cave—and comforting each other had become a burden. There just wasn't anything left to say. There wasn't a month or a year that Bonnie could put her finger on, but somewhere along the way they had started over, each of them somehow finding a way to move on—work, holidays, the garden, everything given a slot.

And there's Janet, of course. Twenty years old and she knows everything. Shacking up with some guy at the first opportunity. Trying too hard to prove she's happy—all that chattering and fidgety laughter during dinner. Bonnie knows happiness shouldn't require effort. It's either there or it isn't. If it isn't, you can't fool anyone. And Bonnie wants to live long enough to have everything come down to simple pleasures, like sitting in the shade watching grandchildren play. But she can't even be certain Janet will get married, let alone have children, not in these times. Both she and Jack are left with all their eggs in one basket. And even if she does marry, Bonnie knows there is no guarantee it will last.

"What in blazes is that guy doin'?" Jack says.

Bonnie edges up on the seat and squints through the windshield. All she can make out are the taillights of the truck that passed them a few minutes ago. They're zig-zagging across the wet road, like a pair of red comets against the black sky. Jack turns on the wipers. Something is on the road. She's about to tell Jack to watch out but he's already slowing down. It's moving toward the ditch but she can't tell if it's an animal or something the wind is blowing. Then she realizes it's a cat, black with white spots on its feet, like tiny socks. She can see it plain as anything, and it's hurt. That truck must have hit it. Suddenly Jack steps on the gas, pulls into the middle of the road and speeds past the wounded animal. Bonnie yells at him to stop as she presses her face to the side window. The cat isn't walking, but writhing on the pavement, its legs jerking into the air.

Again she yells, "Stop the car!"

Air rushes from Jack's nose like a bull fortifying itself. He stares straight ahead, silent, eyes working over every inch of road.

"Jack! You saw that cat didn't you?" She can't believe he went past it. "It needs help. Now stop the car!"

His face remains unchanged, but his lips are quivering like he has something to say but can't get it out.

"I didn't hit it," is all he says.

"Of course you didn't. That truck did. I just want to—"

"You can't help that animal."

"What?"

He snaps his head toward her. "It's dead. Gone."

"No it isn't! I saw with my own eyes. It was alive...and suffering. I can't believe you won't—"

"It's not my fault," he says. "I didn't hit it. It's not my responsibility."

"Are you saying that because you didn't hit it you don't have to help?"

"That's right," he says. "It's only a cat. God made plenty of them."

Bonnie has never known him to be so callous.

"But it's probably some little kid's pet."

"So it's a lesson for the kid. Roads are dangerous. Life is dangerous. Maybe the kid will look both ways before crossing the street."

"But—"

"Listen!" he says, and something piles up in her at the sound of that word, the word he uses when he's about to tell her something he thinks she doesn't know. "Listen. At this very moment, all over the world, animals are getting smacked by cars, buses, trucks, you name it. It can't be stopped."

To Bonnie, everything he's saying is just plain crazy and she's not going to let him get away with it.

"So what if *you* had hit it? Would you stop then?" She doesn't just ask the question, she fires every word at him. Her whole body is shaking.

He doesn't have an answer ready.

"It depends," he finally says.

"Depends! Depends on what?"

"On...how bad it got hit."

"What? Well how do you know that unless you stop?"

"You just sort of feel it," he answers, the last few words are almost impossible to hear. She can tell even he feels stupid saying it.

"Listen!" he growls, his spittle showering across her arms and legs. "I didn't let the damn thing out. I didn't hit—"

"But it's suffering."

"There's nothing new in that."

The car has slowed down—too slow to be on the highway, especially on a night like this. It's as if he can't drive and defend himself at the same time.

"Turn around," she says, the words so final, so flat and direct she doesn't believe they came from her mouth. He looks over at her and for a long moment their eyes lock. And she can't stop thinking that they don't know who they are anymore.

He labours the car to the shoulder, slumps back in his seat and waits. She stares straight ahead, making no attempt to suggest she has anything more to say.

"But it's raining," he finally says, his voice touched with false concern. "You'll get wet."

"It's only water," she says, and it's all she can do to stop from adding: *There's nothing new in that.*

They're both waiting now: Jack, for her to start talking so he can have something to push against; Bonnie, for him to do what she said and turn the car around. The windows begin to fog over; it's like their whole world is about to disappear, and Bonnie doesn't give a damn. She reaches out and pulls the door handle.

"What are you doing?"

"I'm going back," she says. "If you won't drive me, I'll walk."

When she moves to push open the door he throws himself across the seat, grabs the handle and slams the door shut.

"All right! All right!" he hollers. "You win, okay. Are you happy now?" And before she can blink he's cut a violent U-turn without so much as a glance behind him, and they're heading back, straight into the wind.

"Turn on the high beams."

He does what she tells him and they drive up the road in silence, the rain pounding on the windshield.

It's hard to tell where to stop. Bonnie thinks there should be some kind of marks on the road or the shoulder, but now that they're on the other side of the highway, it's difficult to see clearly. Then they pass a mailbox she remembers seeing near the spot. She tells him to turn around and stop.

When she opens the door the wind catches it, pulls it from her hand. She gropes around the car for something to cover herself, but there's nothing. When she steps onto the shoulder of the road her skirt blows up over her waist and her glasses are instantly covered with rain. She takes them off and throws them in the general direction of the dash. Jack is just sitting there looking straight ahead, still as a fossil.

"Are you going to help me?"

He swallows hard once, then nothing. She curses at him and heaves the door closed.

The wind is strong, surprisingly hot, and the rain is not as heavy as she thought, but the drops are huge, the size of bees, and they sting when they hit her bare skin. She gathers her skirt into a ball and begins searching the shoulder where the headlights are shining. She doesn't really know what she's looking for—some kind of tracks, anything. Her mind flashes to the white crosses marking where people have been killed in highway accidents; wreathes of plastic flowers hanging from them. She knows so many people have been killed on this stretch of the road that they'd have to build a sort of tree to hang all the crosses on.

She stands on the edge of the road and looks into the ditch, but it's too dark to see more than a few feet, and without her glasses, it's worse. Everything is in motion. She calls into the swirling darkness, "Here kitty. Come on kitty." She doesn't even know if she's going in the right direction. The cat could be behind her or in the field beyond the ditch. "Here kitty." The wind is so hard she doubts she could hear it even if it did answer.

She looks back at the car, hoping Jack will at least drive forward so she can see better. The dome light inside the car goes on, but she can't see anything else because the headlights are shining right at her. Then his voice, pleading and desperate, blows toward her.

"Please come back to the car."

She yells back, "Why won't you help me?"

"What?"

She cups her hands around her mouth, "Why won't you help me?"

The door slams and the dome light goes off. She waits, expecting to see his body cut in front of the headlights. It doesn't happen.

"Bastard!"

She holds back her hair and starts moving through the ditch, creeping from side to side to cover as much area as possible. "Here kitty." She could step right on it, and the thought of her bare toes brushing against its still-warm body terrifies her. She's soaked right through and feels so useless and stupid she could scream. She surveys the area around her and convinces herself to go as far as the next power pole, telling herself that if nothing turns up, at least she tried, at least she got Jack to do the right thing, even though he didn't so much as get out of the damn car.

Near the pole she trips, hits her toes on something hard and falls into the grass. And even though it doesn't hurt all that much she sits there, amid the broken bottles and garbage, crying. She's crying for the cat, for Janet, for Leah; for being so bloody feeble and clumsy; because her toes hurt and there's mud and gravel stuck in her sandals and God knows what all over her clothes. And she's crying for herself because she doesn't know what else to do.

Then she thinks of Jack, sitting in the car like a goddamn statue. She climbs to the road and limps toward the car, the headlights glaring into her eyes, thinking she'll drag the son of a bitch onto the highway with her bare hands if she has to.

But the headlights are blindingly bright, and when she gets past the front of the car she can't see a bloody thing. Her hand searches for the handle, finds it. The door swings into the wind, almost knocking her onto the road, but Jack isn't there.

She turns off the headlights, and looks up and down the road. She can't see him; she can't see anything. There's a noise in the wind: a low, drawn out note from somewhere behind the car. She walks cautiously, feeling her way beside the car. Her breath is shallow. Her ears isolate every sound. She imagines what sound the cat would make—tiny and high-pitched with lots of air cracking through. She listens for such a sound.

She almost trips over Jack. He's kneeling at the side of the road. She hears the sound again. It's coming from him—a low, dull moan that freezes her where she stands.

The white beam from an approaching car slices through the curve behind them. Jack looks up at her. The car passes along a row of trees and the light from the headlights snaps through the openings, like a flashing strobe. His arms move away from his chest, extend toward her. With each flare of light she struggles to put the fragments together. In his hands, stretching out to her, she makes out the limp body of the cat, whole and showing no outward sign of damage, its white socks waving in the wind. Jack's face is pale, hideous, disgusting; his head bobbing up and down. He's saying something, but all she can hear is the loud heart of her life pounding mercilessly, deep inside her.

The car vaults through the curve, its headlights on high, burning through the rain, through the darkness. She stares into the blinding glare, wishing it would swallow her in its whiteness.

HAPPY

Connie pulls the zipper closed on the Snoopy overnight bag, steps to the back door, and looks out at the kids laughing and chasing each other around the car, and at the apple tree beside the driveway that has always been the earliest tree in the neighbourhood to bear fruit every summer. The apples will be ready soon, and for a moment she wonders if she can just come over and pick some or if she needs to get Dave's permission first. She always liked the apples best when they were just beginning to sweeten. She turns and looks at him, standing in the centre of the kitchen in that slumping pose he's acquired over the last few years, the same harsh expression on his face that he still had difficulty defending. She could never help feeling something toward him, though she never could figure out what, or even why she took the trouble. She worried about him, pitied him, loved him and hated him all at the same time. It must be the kids, she told herself. As long as we share the kids I'll always see his lonely shadow standing at the edge of my life. Even the divorce hadn't freed her. She makes a mental note to avoid the apple question, for now.

"So," she starts, slipping her fingers into the pockets of her cut-offs, pulling herself to full height, "are you happy?"

Dave recognizes her pattern of asking questions she's not really sure she wants answered; how she asks them only after planning some escape route such as the now-opened back door. Near the end of the marriage he noticed how often she would roll down the car window and holler one last statement toward the house as she drove away, as if there were something to be won by getting in the last insult. He doesn't answer right away and takes a second to consider the word "happy," testing it for possibilities.

"Well," he finally says, quite matter-of-factly, "lately I've been trying not to qualify how I feel."

She hadn't thought about what he might say, but the instant it came out it sounded like the only possible thing he could have said. A pure Daveism. A pure load of nothing. "God!" she says. "Isn't that just like you!"

The corner of Dave's mouth curls upward, but she knows him too well to mistake it for a smile.

"I want to avoid thinking about how I feel all the time. Life is complicated enough without having to qualify it."

She wants to laugh and cry at the same time. "But aren't you doing what you want?"

"Yeah. I guess so." His tone is purposefully flat, methodical, overly rational, as if each word is chosen by some high-ordered thought process and he's reserving the right to recall anything without notice. "But that doesn't mean I have to be happy. I might be glad to be doing it, but not necessarily happy *while* I'm doing it."

He checks her eyes to see if she's following or just humouring him. She holds his glance, nods slowly like she hasn't yet made up her mind and leans her back against the doorjamb.

"If you ask me if I have a sore throat or a headache, I can answer, no problem. But even if you say 'Are you sick?' we're into relative terms."

"Dave, it's just a simple quest—"

"If I say I'm not sick, does that mean I couldn't be any healthier? Even people who are sick as dogs usually say they're fine. Nobody wants an honest answer."

"Sometimes they do."

"It's just habit. And anyway, what does happiness really mean?"

"You've got me there," she answers. "Someone once said people tend to make themselves as happy as they want."

"I like that. Can I use it?"

"It's not mine to give away."

"Yeah, well, there you go," he says. "We're back to language, ownership, the illusion of meaning. One man's goose is another man's gander. We might as well be talking about dipsies and doodles." He shrugs his shoulders, as if whatever he just said has completed some kind of circle.

Connie crosses her arms over her chest and stares down at the linoleum. The pattern is too familiar.

Dave walks to the sink, places his hands on the counter and looks out the window. He knows he'd never be able to keep his mouth shut; he knows he doesn't have a chance.

"I'm sick of hearing everything in black and white," he says, gazing into the neighbour's yard. "Abortion. Quebec. God. No one wants to think anymore. I figure the theologians can take the blame for much of it."

"I don't see what you mean," she says, and it's only after the words escape her mouth that she realizes what she's done. She wants to kick herself for not seeing it building, expanding toward her like a dark hole: the ranting and swearing; his face either red from trying to find some esoteric word buried in his brain or pale with depression; his constant analysis of television, movies, the books she read to the kids and everything else that she'd once been able to sit back and enjoy. She's being swept into it again, as if she had never been away. The sleepless nights, the newspapers he'd crush into a ball and throw across the room; his unrelenting disgust with magazines and movie stars; the light like a fire burning under the door of the study until dawn; the kids having to tiptoe around the house. If only his parents hadn't left such a large inheritance; if only he hadn't quit his job with Greyhound; if only he'd never gone to that goddamn university. But it's too late now. He's already going on about the way people form their opinions as if they were buying tubes of toothpaste, and that choices are the only real power people have. She knows all he needed was someone to stand in one place long enough to make him think he had an audience. If it weren't for the kids spending time with him, she doubts he'd ever get out of the house.

He hears his voice change gears as he launches into the way people reduce everything into either yes or no, good or bad, and to hell with whatever is in-between. How he's sick of all those menial minds spouting someone else's idea of truth, sick of newspapers written for the average grade-nine reader, sick of bumpersticker solutions to complex problems. But he doesn't tell her about the voice in his head. How the phrase *the necessary Judas* keeps repeating itself over and over like a jingle from an ad slogan, a hook in a pop song. And he doesn't tell her that whenever he hears it he imagines a worm crawling around in his skull, eating through his brain, creating a labyrinth of tunnels that will someday cause his mind to fold in on itself, collapse into nothingness; and that he's desperate to work the phrase into some kind of idea that equates the whole notion of opposites and absolutes with wives' tales and old-world thought. He's looking for a synthesis of heaven and hell, morality and degradation, some kind of psychic trickster to redeem the Western mind. He keeps thinking about Judas, how he was set up to take the rap, and that it had to be done. He wants to get into Judas' mind, see the whole story, find out everything all at once. But he can't find the door, the crack, a fault he can wedge himself through. He knows there's a wall somewhere, but he can't tell if it's locking him out or holding him in. And all the while the worm keeps burrowing.

"I just don't think we're meant to be happy," he says. "Meant to feel like we really belong where we are."

"Well that's a real comfort, Dave."

"And once you know why you always feel like a piece of shit, then you've really found something. You don't have to like it, but at least you're free of all the bullshit and guilt."

She shakes her head and looks out to the car. She can't see the kids but she can hear them playing on the tire-swing in the corner of the yard. It's still bright and clear outside. She can see for miles down the valley.

"Dave?" she says, turning back to him. "You're a very depressing person. You should get out of the house more often. Go fishing or something like you used to. Maybe find a—"

"I don't need your advice! It's all those people with smiles carved on their faces who need help." He starts pacing the kitchen, throwing his arms in jagged, uneven gestures, warding off some invisible assailant. "Don't you get it? We're supposed to be disappointed. Happiness is abnormal."

Connie pushes herself free of the wall. She's heard it all before. She'll put up with his tirades for a few minutes, mostly because she no longer has to put up with him at all.

One of the kids starts crying.

"I have to go," she says. "Thanks for taking the kids."

He shrugs and follows her out the door. When he gets to the steps he stops and watches as Connie gathers the kids into the car, both of them voicing some minor grievance as she buckles them in. She hasn't changed very much in eleven years, a little heavier, but he always liked the extra weight. It made her look substantial, vital, nothing like those formula bodies every man was supposed to drool over. Her hair is nearly blonde from the summer sun. In a month or so he knows she'll colour it with a rinse to hide the dark roots, then just before Christmas she'll have it cut short again for the winter.

He's successfully managed to drive her away again.

"Still taking the kids in two weeks?" she asks as she starts the engine.

"What? Oh, yeah. Sure. Two weeks. I'll phone you."

She nods and begins to back down the driveway, then stops and looks back at him, through him, wondering just where he is at all. She leans out the window. "Dave?"

"Yeah."

He moves toward her, his body still drooped forward, the sombre eyes fixing on her like a target. Her foot is already off the brake. "Never mind," she says, and the car lurches to the street.

His son waves out the side window as they drive away. Dave lifts an arm and tries to manage a smile.

Dave remains standing in the driveway for a long time—long enough for the first star to become faintly visible. The corner of his mouth curls upward when he sees it. He knows it's not a star, not an object, but a wave of energy millions of light-years old—a sign from a past that existed before life, yet announcing itself every night for the first time. He remembers when he used to believe stars were holes in some enormous barrier that surrounded the earth like a plastic bag. And beyond that barrier there was only one great light that shone on everything. But Dave is no longer fooled by a child's dream.

He moves along the driveway, feeling the day's accumulated heat rising from the pavement. Beside the apple tree he notices some of the leaves have curled and gone brown, and he remembers he has forgotten to spray for caterpillars. He wonders what would happen if he just left the tree alone. How much chaos can a few caterpillars cause? And besides, it's not as if he needs five hundred pounds of apples. He reaches high into the branches and picks the biggest apple he can find, rolls it in his hands. The skin is smooth and tight—no scabs, no blemishs, no wormholes. It's perfect despite his negligence, or—and he can't stop smiling—perhaps because of it. He brings it to his mouth and bites deeply, enjoying the crisp cracking of the skin and pulp. His mouth fills with bitter juice. The insides of his cheeks contract. His whole body shutters. But his jaws continue their slow and deliberate rhythm. He swallows and bites again.

The remnants of a once happy family are now far away, pressing toward other temporary futures. Dave continues to read and think in his study, taking more classes at the university, trying to chart his way through the voices in his mind. He is a common man with a common mind and a not-so-common desire to ponder himself into trouble. He will always be burdened with the phrase *the necessary Judas,* and his ex-wife will often be heard saying he spent too much time thinking and not enough time living.

Dave is often seen, weekends and summers, in local parks and at the zoo. He has his children with him. He has become a member of the permanent part-time fathers of North America. He buys ice cream and rides at the fair. As he listens to their stories he is tempted to defend himself, and occasionally, to turn his children against their mother. And he struggles to do neither. Instead, he tells them people are very complex, and life is a tangle of complications, and most of the time it's the chaos that takes over and not the people. Whenever he speaks like this his kids look at him with the same questioning expression their mother would have. And despite everything he has tried so hard to believe, he will want them to be happy.

In his sleep he often stumbles upon the wall. Darkness is every-where. He must feel his way forward, tripping over roots, leafless branches scratching his face, fingers probing the cold stones. And there, suddenly, a narrow shaft of light cutting through the vacant dark, lighting him with wonder and possibility. Alone, always alone in this dream, he reaches out, touching the vibrant edge of the mystery. And then he will fall and weep over the smallness of the light and the cruel dark path that brought him here.

SCARS

S even thirty-five in the evening is an innocent hour to answer a phone. It's Teddy.

"I've got some bad news," she says. She sounds duty-bound, controlled, factual, the usual forced inflections she has mastered over the years—as though making the call is another responsibility that only she, being the oldest sibling, can handle. But despite the familiar voice, the picture of her face instantly falling into place, it seems the voice of a stranger, an intruder. It's a struggle to stop myself from slamming the phone down. Words drift like water through a net. I catch only a few of them: *Dad...heart attack...kitchen.* Bad news requires little effort to understand. I would have been more prepared to hear her say it was Mom who had died.

What to feel? A part of me stands off to the side, commenting on every thought and movement: *He doesn't look very strong... He can't think himself through something like this... Notice how his arms hang limp at his side.* The comments play overtop of each other like a recording, wrestling to be heard. Sometime later, Claire finds me sitting in the dark on the corner of our bed. I don't remember going here.

In the plane I keep thinking about time, how it seems to have meaning only when something like this happens. Its trick is to hide behind the flow of each day running into the next. Then something happens—a wedding, a birth, someone dies—and all at once those days become years, decades. At that moment it's not how far you've come or what you've achieved that matters, but what hasn't changed, what you haven't done. Time is supposed to be the greatest healer. I'd like to believe that, like to believe in something simple enough to be said in a single breath. Time the healer; time the deceiver. Take your pick.

But memories do fade. You see shadows where there once were trees. There are details, here and there—a date, a neighbour's name, a piece of furniture. They tumble toward you like photographs falling from a scrapbook, but the pictures seem to belong to someone else's life. The shadows never really regain substance, but they never completely disappear either. Some impression remains, half visible, shifting or staying still, a dark current under ice. There are rooms in a distant corner of my mind. I check the doors often, making certain everything is secure. This scar on the middle finger of my right hand: a jagged white band circling the knuckle. Even in the dull light of the plane it glares against the surrounding skin. I keep it hidden, try to avoid looking at it.

We're just breaking over the eastern edge of the Rockies. Outside everything is shrouded in grey. Clouds lie beneath the plane: huge, stratified sheets of mist. Nothing is truly black or white. In places I can see through them enough to notice the changes in the terrain, but not enough to recognize anything. Even where there's a break in the cloud, and a clear view of what I know are the foothills, there's nothing but a mass of grey upon grey. Even the wing of the plane is barely visible in this colourless world.

A focus, that's what I need. Something to keep the doors from opening.

I try to figure out the age of everyone in the family. There's order in counting...safety of numbers. Carrie is six years older than me, so that makes her forty-eight. Then Teddy, she'd be fifty-one, no, fifty-two. Jesus. Fifty-two. I have a sister fifty-two years old? The ten-year difference seems like an entire generation. How can you compare Bobby Rydel to Hendrix? Betty Crocker to hash brownies? I can hear Teddy's voice; feel her condemning stare. My stomach tightens at the thought of walking back into that house and having to put up with her "Ricky" shit again: "Ricky, get Mom a coffee. Ricky do this. Ricky do that." Christ, I can take Richard or Rich, but I haven't been "Ricky" for twenty-five years. The moment I walk in the door all she'll see is "Ricky the asshole. Ricky the Punk." Someone who's still a kid who can't control his temper. Someone you don't turn your back on. So much for numbers and closed doors.

Everything is still washed in grey as the plane begins its descent. The orderly pattern of street lights gradually emerges. A hint of colour from the roofs of houses. And then the bright red and blue of a Wal-Mart sign pushes out of the gloom, as large and definable as anything I've ever seen.

Wal-Mart. Saskatoon. Home?

The accordion exit ramp has broken down and we have to leave the plane by way of a set of stairs butted up to the door. Everyone is busy complaining about the cold. Inside, I find a phone and call the house. Carrie answers. At least it's not Teddy. She tries to hide her surprise that I'm in town and asks if someone should come to pick me up. She sounds more relaxed when I tell her I'll take a cab and be staying with friends. When she asks if I want to see Dad, the first thought that comes to me is how hard she must be taking it. Then I wonder if she's trying some kind of twisted humour on me.

I'm about to remind her he's dead when she says the name of the funeral home, and I realize she's asking me if I want to view the body. View the body! It never occurred to me. Do I want to see the body of my dead father? What the hell kind of question is that? She waits for a second, then repeats the name of the place, saying it's up to me and it's open until eight. I change the subject.

"How's Mom doing?"

"It's hard to tell; she's hardly stopped sobbing since the last stroke...the one she had in September." She can't conceal the admonishment in her voice, as if Mom's condition is a complete mystery to me. "And when anyone says anything to her she starts again. She won't get out of bed..." It all comes out like a recorded message meant for anybody and nobody. "The stroke did something to her brain. She gets her words mixed around. She blames herself for what happened to Dad, all the work he had to do because of her, that's what Teddy says. She says Mom wants to give up."

I cut in and lie about someone wanting to use the phone, then tell her I'll be at the house later.

Do I want to see Dad?

Outside the terminal the question keeps turning through my head, a voice in a dream I don't wish to have. When the cab driver asks, "Where to?" the voice repeats the name of the funeral home. I sit like a prisoner in the back seat as the taxi heads into town.

A short man with a manicured smile and careful eyes appears at the door.

"Are you a member of the family?"

When he reaches to shake my hand I want to knock his ass to the floor and leave.

"Yes," I say, quickly releasing my hand from his. "He was...is my Dad."

He nods knowingly, professionally, motions me forward. An arm curves around my back, guiding me down the corridor, into a room. The door closes softly behind me, the click of the latch hanging in the air.

I don't see it so much as feel its weight tilting the floor like the deck of a ship. I look straight ahead, then to my left, searching for diversion, ballast: the yellow glow of recessed lights; the pastel autumn-orange walls; the thick, cream-coloured carpet. At the far end are two upholstered, straight-back chairs and a small round table between them. A vase with pink and white carnations. A brass tissue box. From hidden speakers violins and cellos weave sleepily in search of a melody, medicating the air with softness. Two matched paintings strike me as being out of place. What kind of solace is there in flowering valleys and misty mountains for people from Saskatchewan? There are no walls on the prairie, only air and space and light; the promised land the horizon, a thin line forever receding.

I turn to the polished box.

His face is pale and dry. Hair neatly combed. Fingernails clipped and filed. So this is what death looks like. I'm tempted to lift the closed end of the coffin to see if they've gone to the trouble of putting shoes and socks on him. Everything seems to be out of a movie and I half expect him to suddenly reach out, grab my arm and start hollering. They've dressed him in the only suit I've ever seen him wear, the one Mom made him buy for Carrie's wedding. He doesn't fill the jacket now. The tie looks new, blue with thin silver stripes. Probably purchased for the occasion.

The hands seem to belong to some other body. These ones are smooth and innocent as a baby's. No hint of grease or dirt etched into the creases, under the nails. But the tendons are there, stretching like steel cables along the tops on his hands; and then the hard mass of muscle rising between the base of his thumb and first finger. There's stubble on his chin—a wino asleep in the park. It's broken through the make-up and flecks of powder have fallen on his collar and down his neck. Then the scar. On his bottom lip. A half inch line no beard could conceal. They've tried to hide it with make-up. That would be Teddy's doing. I imagine her pointing to it; whispering instructions to the undertaker.

An image rushes forward. There's swearing; hands on my shoulders. The kitchen light. Mom's voice. Crying. Yelling. I can't make out the words. The hands squeeze into my shoulders, shaking me, forcing me to the floor. I make a fist and throw it out in front of me. I throw it with all my strength.

I had always believed it wasn't a fist that was aimed. It was simply hurled out into space, something random, wild. But this time it's different. This time I see it being guided toward the jaw. I feel the sharp contact, the sinking satisfaction of having hit the mark. The look of surprise. The blood bursting from his mouth. The hands sliding from my shoulders as he wobbles, staggers backward. And then the sneer cutting across my face.

It's all there. It's always been there. I've watched this scene hundreds of times, but now there's this unexpected twist, this short clip spliced in. For the first time I have no doubt what my intentions were.

A deadening ache floods my right hand. It's rising. Moving of its own power, the white knuckle trembling as it nears his face. Then gently, two feathers, they come together.

I'm not much for crowds and small talk. I need to get out of this house, away from the red eyes, pallid faces and sighs. I have no intention of becoming familiar with funeral etiquette.

I grab my coat and make my way through the blue cigarette smoke in the kitchen, glancing up to Mom's room as I pass the stairs. They're both still standing in the dim light outside her door, whispering. Teddy is saying something and Carrie is nodding her head slowly, like a nun praying. They look up without interrupting themselves. My eyes settle for a moment on Carrie. I know Teddy is talking about me, and it's easy to see Carrie agrees with whatever she's saying. Half an hour and they still haven't said a word to me. I head for the door.

It's not too cold for a winter night in Saskatchewan, but I'm no longer used to it. The three evergreens lining the driveway sag under the weight of snow, as though they, too, are mourning some kind of loss. It doesn't seem that long ago when Dad planted them. I must have been eleven or twelve. I catch myself again when I realize that was over thirty years ago.

It feels good to be in the cold, to have some real yet mindless obstacle to defend against. My skin tightens against the stinging breeze and I'm relieved, even glad, to endure it. My parents' house is lit up as if a party is going on inside. A few strands of Christmas lights glow here and there along the empty street. The sidewalk is buried under smooth waves of snow, a sea of motionless cloud. I'd forgotten how dry, how light, prairie snow is; it seems weightless against my plowing feet.

A vehicle is slowing behind me, and as I stop to look a city bus pulls up to where I'm standing. Then I notice the sign on the post in front of me. But it's too late, the door is already opening. The next thing I know I'm walking up the steps. It's not that I decided to go anywhere. But it's a lot easier to just get in the bus than it would be to tell the driver he stopped for nothing.

"How much?" I ask, busily searching for my wallet to cover my embarrassment.

"Dollar and a half," he says in a friendly voice. The door closes and we pull away.

I pass him two dollars.

He looks at it, and then at me, as if something more than money has been revealed. "Sorry, I can't make change," he says.

I tell him it doesn't matter and make my way down the aisle. He must have been hoping for some company. It seems a lonely job on a night like this. Can't even listen to a radio.

The bus is empty, but throbbing with brutal fluorescent light. I squint to cut the glare and take the first seat behind the back door, the same place I always sat as a kid. When was the last time I rode a bus? Must be twenty years or more. Nothing seems to have changed, though, except the ads above the windows. Instead of pushing breath mints and fashion magazines they're now geared to information on AIDS, crisis lines, teen pregnancy. Everywhere there are pictures of kids on crutches, in wheelchairs, phone numbers of agencies specializing in the distress of your choice. Aside from this everything looks just as I remember—even the sickly two-tone green walls and seats.

The driver is eyeing me in the mirror again. We've gone only a few blocks and it's the third time I've caught him doing it. When he sees me look at him he doesn't turn away. Maybe we went to the same high school, or played on some team together and he's trying to place me. Claire says I still look like I did when we met, twenty years ago. I get the feeling he's about to say something. I turn and stare out the window. I don't live here anymore.

I can't recall most of the streets. I remember some names— Munroe, Ruth, Cascade—but I'm lost trying to give most of them a place. The bus stops, turns right, and for the first time I'm able to put a name to a street. When I was a kid, this bus route went down Clarence, crossed the river, through the city core, then across the river again and back up Broadway. Its circuit made the shape of a horseshoe, the unconnected parts being about half a mile from each other at the extreme south end of its route, which is where I was standing when the bus stopped. I could ask the driver if the route is still the same, but then he'll start asking who I am, where I'm from and God knows what else.

Taylor Street. So the next one will be Eighth. Bowman High. Teddy and Carrie went there. Probably still full of Jensen-sweater type kids, yesteryear's spoiled brats. The old B/A station, where I used to watch the pumps for Jim while he slipped over to the plaza to buy us beer. Now it's a red-and-white-striped fried chicken place. That school. What's it called? Winston? Williston?

The houses become smaller and older as the bus moves through the quiet night, past the pre-World War II houses with windowed verandas, sagging wooden steps; the river's surface stilled with ice; the wind curling at the corners of empty downtown streets. There's nothing out there that links me to the past or the present.

Love? I guess that's what it's called. Being able to bend and forgive, that's the hardest. I can forgive him, that's the easy part. It's my own forgiveness I can't handle. How do I offer myself something like that?

This will be the end of the line if we turn at the next corner. When I hear the driver turn on the signal light I slide across the seat and stand. He glances at me in the mirror, then looks away. I could stay on the bus and ride it all the way around again, but I've decided to get off here and walk the mile back to the house. It seems time to make some sort of decision.

"You getting off here?" he asks as I approach. Again, he looks in the mirror, eyes still searching.

"Yeah," I say. "I guess so."

The bus comes to a stop and the door opens. I'm halfway down the steps before I realize he has said something else. I stop and look back.

"You okay?" he says.

The words don't seem to have anything to do with me. I look down at the floor, as if the answer just fell from my pocket. There's nothing there. The driver leans over the steering wheel, his head twisted toward me. He's in no hurry for an answer, but he wants one. Words buzz through my head, but none of them connect. I could stand here all night and still not know what to answer. The windshield wipers sweep back and forth, measuring the fullness of my silence.

"I don't know," I finally say. It's the only honest answer I can think of. I step into the cold, aware of how pathetic my response must seem. I feel his eyes watching as I walk away.

When I get to the corner the bus still hasn't moved. The white fluorescent interior radiates onto the surrounding snow. There are no details visible inside the bus; everything has been consumed by light. The door is still open.

The wind has stopped now. Snowflakes, some of them the size of leaves, glide through the air, changing course every few seconds as if free to choose their own destination. It's like being in one of those glass bubbles, the winter scene with a snowman, evergreens and deer, after it's been shaken then placed on a coffee table. I stand inside the circle of a street light, close my eyes and listen to the frozen quiet. I want to hear a coyote cry into the still air; a grouse breaking from beneath the white surface. I could be anywhere in this moment, any place where there is only winter and dark and the possibility of sound. I keep my eyes closed and slide through the weightless waves. It becomes a game, something a child would do. I'm a blind man, lost in a winter storm. I get a rhythm going: ten sliding steps, a quick look, and then repeat it. "One... Two... Three." Each number filled with purpose. "Four... Five... Six." My voice growing louder with each step. "Seven... Eight..."

I take a shortcut through the school grounds. Away from the

street the snowflakes appear to be self-illuminated. They glow and twinkle like fireflies. There's a skating rink behind the school. I walk over to look at the ice, maybe slide around on it.

A dark, baggy shape lies on the far end of the rink. A dog or maybe someone's parka. The closer I get the less it looks like an abandoned coat. A pair of short legs—a grey boot on one, a black one on the other. A thin stream of hoar-frost rises from the opposite end of the coat. I run forward.

An old man lies crumpled on the ice, his face flat against the frozen surface, a small pool of blood puddled by his forehead. I lie belly-down on the ice. Look at his face.

His eyes open, focus on my coat, then move slowly to my face. "Who are you?" he asks, his voice guarded.

I ask if he's all right. He thinks for a second, then says, "I fell down."

"Yes."

"Not so smart for an old man, eh?"

"Your forehead. It's cut."

He doesn't seem concerned.

"I'll put some ice on it," he says. A definite smile spreads across his lips. His eyes brighten.

"How do you feel? Can you move?"

"I feel fine."

He seems to be all right. I ask him what the date is. He looks at me curiously, then in a blunt voice says, "Winter." Again the smile. A soft laughter passes between us.

"I think I better get you home."

He reaches out and grabs the arm of my coat. The strength of his grip surprises me.

"No," he says. "Not yet. I like it here. It's quiet. I like the cold, it makes me feel good."

"Your family must be worried about you."

He ignores me.

"What's your name?" he asks.

"Richard. Richard Graham."

His eyes narrow as he searches my face, but a moment later they begin to cloud over. He removes his hand from my coat, reaches across and gently brushes the snow from my hair. He smiles again, then asks if I have a car. I tell him I do but it's not here. He asks what kind it is. He seems keen on knowing.

"It's a Subaru." He says he never heard of it.

I tell him it's made in Japan and he frowns.

"Should'a bought a Buick," he says. "I bought Buicks all the time. They're big. People get out of your way when you have a big car."

He starts rambling about the cars he's owned, trips he and his wife have taken: Vancouver, Jasper, Seattle.

A young voice is calling from the street, "Grampa! Grampa!" I get the old man moving. He's still talking about Buicks, the Rockies, green water, glaciers. The paintings in the funeral home pop into my mind, and then a girl running at the edge of the school grounds spots us. Her excited yells echo across the field as she dashes forward. We shuffle to the side of the rink. He's not very sure on his feet, and neither am I. I wrap my arm around his waist; he reaches for my hand. The girl's parents suddenly appear, and in a few seconds they're all in a circle, hugging and chastizing the old man, expressing thanks, relief. The girl's mother apologizes and mouths the word "Alzheimer's" while the old man mumbles about having just gone for a walk—no reason to worry about a man going for a walk.

As they group together and walk away, the old man stops to look back at me. He raises his hand and waves a finger in my direction. His face folds in frustration. He's trying to remember something, but it's gone. He shakes his head, sighs, then looks down at the worried face of his granddaughter. His hand comes down and tussles her hair; then resting it on her shoulder, they turn and walk away.

Nothing has changed: the bare and twisted shrubs; the branches of the evergreens drooping under the weight of snow. There's no light on in Mom's room, but there's a dull orange glow in the kitchen window. I walk up the driveway noticing the footprints that have come and gone in the snow. Mine are in there somewhere, mixed in with friends of the family, relatives, Dad's buddies from the Legion. From the steps I can hear muted voices, the sound of dishes being washed. Someone is stirring coffee and the rapid clinking of the spoon tells me it's Teddy. She's probably talking to Carrie about what to do with Mom: whether she should be placed in a home or moved in with one of them; whether the house should be sold, rented; what to do with the furniture. Teddy will make all the decisions now that Dad's gone. She'll be the one to decide what to keep, who's in and who's out. I listen closely, trying to hear my name. But their voices are only a murmur.

The old man. He must be home by now, wrapped in a blanket, cup of tea in hand. Maybe Mom knows who he is. For all I know he could've been living here long before our house was built. I suppose nothing has changed for him either—probably already forgot my name. Alzheimer's. I wonder what else he's forgotten. Maybe that funny look in his eyes means he's been set free, that whatever he's regretted doing or not doing no longer has a claim on him.

The storm door knocks softly against the entry, a slight rattle from the loose and worn down hinges. The door needs to be painted again. I can still see the scratches from our failed attempt at having a family dog—a short-haired terrier, with more energy than brains, that hated winter and hid under my bed whenever it was time to go outside. As soon as he was out of the house he would howl and jump against the door and drive everyone crazy. By the time he was three there was nothing anyone could do to stop him from humping every pillow in the house. Then one day the dog was gone. Whenever we asked about him Dad would just shrug his shoulders. In the end, we were all glad to be rid of him.

I suppose it's time for a new door. A metal one this time. I could go to the hardware store first thing in the morning. I inhale a breath of cold air, pulling it deep into my lungs, holding it there as I reach for the door.

ACTS OF FORGIVENESS

As soon as I walked into the house, Brucie called me over to the table to show me the paper mask he made at playschool. I could hear Deb on the phone in the bedroom. Brucie waved a piece of crayon covered paper in the air. There were two holes cut out for eye slots and an elastic band stapled to the back. "He's a clown," said Brucie. "A scary clown." The sound of Deb's voice was unusual, not alarming or panic-filled, but sort of flighty, eager one minute, then low, almost mumbling the next. "Could you spell that for me?" I heard her say. Then she repeated a phone number.

Brucie managed to pull the mask over his face; his eyes were nowhere near the holes. "Grr-ah!" he said, sounding suprisingly scary and funny at the same time.

When Deb finally came into the kitchen she was flushed with happiness.

"Good news?" I asked.

"The best," she said, sweeping Brucie into her arms, kissing his neck, dancing toward the living room while he pretended to complain. "Carl! We found Carl!" Her eyes were glazing over.

"Carl who?"

"Carl, my brother. Brucie has a new uncle!" She removed the mask from his face, crushed the boy closer and spun toward the couch.

"Unkie! Unkie!" squealed Brucie.

Carl, the long-lost brother. The last remnant of her family. She hadn't mentioned him for a couple of years.

"Really? That's great. So, fill me in."

"A woman called this morning. Norma something, I've got it written down, from Missoula, Montana." She sat down, our son now happily giving in to her bear hug. "I've been on the phone all day. Can you believe it, he's still in Montana? Said she was calling on behalf of Carl. 'Carl?' I said. Then she said, 'Morehouse, Carl Morehouse.' Then I thought, oh no, he's dead. My little brother, dead."

She hadn't seen or heard from him since she was twelve or thirteen. That would be close to twenty years ago.

"Your little brother must be what, twenty-six? Twenty-seven?"

"She had phoned half the Morehouses in the state before finding one who knew anything about my adoption, the new name, moving to Canada. It must have been someone we met when we went down there last, when I was pregnant with Brucie."

That was when she found the orphanage had been levelled and replaced with a retirement complex. All the nuns had gotten too old; the last recruit to the order arrived in the late 1960s.

"So he's fine, after all. All grown up. There you go. He survived the orphanage. Did he find a foster family? Was he adopted?"

"I don't know. We'll have to go visit. I didn't get to talk to him yet."

"But you've been on the phone all day."

"Yes. But not with him."

"Oh?"

"Carl's in jail."

Brian was good about letting me take a few days off, especially considering how busy we were. The whole town had been on a big swing upward for the last year. People were moving in from all over the country: loggers, miners, tradesmen. Pulp and paper mills were running three shifts a day, and a big copper concern was about to go into production a few miles out of town. We had framing jobs lined up from April right into Christmas, and we'd been going flat out, ten hours a day, all summer. I was what we call a highballer, someone who doesn't waste time, who knows all the tricks, someone who puts the job ahead of himself. I hadn't missed a day all summer, and I had no intention to until this Carl business came up. The money had never been better. I had my eye on a lot on the edge of town, thinking that if the work stayed steady, and if we started small—two bedrooms, one bathroom, nothing fancy—we'd have a shot at our own place. It's what Deb always wanted, always needed: a home to live in, not just a house; some stable place where she could arrange her own world. I hadn't mentioned anything to her, it was going to be a surprise. But now, with finding her brother, the next few months were really going to be something.

In the days before leaving for Montana, Deb lived with the phone stuck to her ear, arranging times and talking to the authorities about what could and couldn't happen when she saw Carl: How long could they visit? Could she give him anything? Were there ever any exceptions to the rules? The whole time she was hoping they would give her some kind of concession for the two of them being separated so long. She spent hours talking to this Norma woman, who, it turned out, was one of those people who strikes up letter-writing relationships with prisoners, for what reason I have no idea. Apparently, after writing to Carl for some time, she visited him in jail, where she was convinced to try to find Deb. Even though Norma seemed to know next to nothing about Carl, Deb started to use her as a messenger to ask him certain questions about his past, so she could try to fill in the blanks while we made plans to visit. It seemed odd that Carl had this stranger do something he could have done any time over the last ten years. If a perfect stranger could find Deb in a matter of weeks, why couldn't Carl have tracked her down years ago? But there was no use bringing this stuff up to Deb, at least not yet, not when we were a hair away from meeting the guy. It was Deb's time to celebrate.

By noon on Wednesday we had deposited Brucie with my folks and were headed south, to Montana, Carl, and the beginning of Deb's life. She was an adult now, not a kid; a mother, not an orphan like Carl. I knew she wouldn't be able to stop herself from acting as if her little brother had fallen under her care, that she would feel as duty-bound to worry over Carl as much as she worried over Brucie. She was a woman who woke up every day wanting to be the kind of mother she'd never had: patient, dependable, protective, sober; the kind of mother who always had fresh bread in the oven.

On the trip south Deb gradually revealed what she had been able to patch together about Carl.

"So he borrowed some furniture...," I asked.

"A table and two chairs. Old stuff, sitting out on the back lawn for weeks."

"...but forgot to ask for permission."

"He assumed they were left behind when someone moved out."

I was starting to get the feeling I was listening to a twelve year old's version of events. Deb had already acquired the habit of being Carl's defender, and after all she'd been through, the last thing I wanted to do was sound suspicious.

"Doesn't sound like something that would put anyone in jail," I said. "Couldn't he just set everything straight with the neighbour? Give the furniture back? Apologize?"

"And then there was a misunderstanding when the police wanted to look around his suite." She was picking her words carefully. "He'd had a few bad days in a row at the time. He knew he didn't have to let them in, and told them so. It's not as if he killed someone. You know how cops can be. Everyone has bad days. He just opened his mouth at the wrong time."

"So he lipped off the cops, who also just happened to be having a bad day?"

"Yeah, something like that."

"And the next thing he knew he was in the cruiser—"

"And the guy who owned the furniture said it's worth over five hundred bucks, which Carl says is what the cops told him to say because that means the charges are more serious."

She obviously wasn't capable of seeing Carl as anything other than an innocent victim. Either the cops in the States were real screwballs or this guy must have done something to set all this nonsense in motion.

"So you're basically saying the cops are so pissed at Carl they want to see him fry."

"I don't know," she said. For the first time since receiving the phone call the glow that had surrounded her darkened, and it was because of me.

"I'm sorry," I said, giving her hand a squeeze. "Let's just wait and see. We really don't know anything, right?"

"Yeah, right." She nodded. And then she did this miraculous thing only she can do.

She leaned back, her head falling against the headrest, eyes closed. It was like a Zen thing, I guess, some kind of homemade fast-serve meditation she had invented long before we met. With each breath the glow began to return. She had told me once that what she does is organize her world from the inside out, by imagining what it will feel like when something wonderful comes to completion. Visualization, that's what they call it nowadays. It was a carry-over from the orphanage, when she'd imagine the day her mother would come back for her and Carl, the drugs and prostitution and basement apartments long gone. Now she was seeing just herself and Carl, the two of them together again. Then she smiled, her grin growing in length, moving beyond her lips, taking control; the final transformation.

"Hey," I said. She opened her eyes and rolled her head toward me. "Brucie has a new uncle."

At the border Deb jokingly told the U.S. customs officer she had dual citizenship, being born in Montana then becoming a Canadian citizen when she was twenty-four. The customs officer said they didn't recognize dual citizenship in the States, that if she was born in the U.S. she'd always be an American, then added, "Why would anyone want to be anything else?" It was the kind of statement I always found remarkable for its loyalty, yet equally terrifying for the same reason.

We pulled off the road and slept in the van that night, about an hour past the border. I had roughed-in a bed by the back doors the summer before, for just such a purpose. Mid-afternoon the next day we arrived at the jail, a multi-storey stone building in the heart of Missoula. After ten minutes of filling out forms, then waiting another twenty minutes, we were sent into a visiting room that was pretty much right out of a movie. The windows were high on the walls, so you couldn't look out, and were covered with a heavy wire mesh. Nothing but flat, hard surfaces everywhere. And they must have gotten a deal on blue paint because everything—the floor, ceiling, even the desks and chairs—was the same colour: a world without choice. In places there were what looked like one-inch thick globs of blue glue hardened on the walls, as if they simply blew up a vat of paint in the centre of the room. A glass wall sectioned into cubicles separated the far third of the room. Half of the visiting stations were occupied, mostly by women, some of them prison groupies like Norma, no doubt, and a couple of lawyer-types in suits. It was no place to meet a lost brother, or anyone for that matter. We stood in the open centre of the room, like lost tourists, staring at the glass wall, not knowing what to do. Was Carl in the room or still on his way? We didn't even know who to look for.

A door opened on the other side of the glass wall, and a fairly large man walked in. He was dressed in what looked like blue pajamas, the same blue as the room. Deb started, as if to wave or run forward, then stopped. He had what I would call a sort of beach-boy face because of his blond hair and how it was pointing in all directions, like he'd just come out of the wind. The man looked at us and nodded his head at Deb, as if asking a question. If he was Carl, Deb seemed to be having a hard time convincing herself. She moved forward uncertainly, the two of them reaching the open cubicle at the same time. Like I said, he was a big man, over six feet and around two hundred and ten pounds. I wouldn't say he was fat or even muscular, though, but puffy, bloated, like there was a uniform layer of water under his skin. Deb grabbed the phone off the wall.

"Carl! Carl!" She must have caught something familiar about him. She opened her hand and pressed it to the glass. He gave her a cock-eyed smile, his mouth closed but running at an odd angle. The kind of smile you see on old men who have lost all their teeth.

Deb was crying before he had his phone off the hook. His hand came up and spread over the glass opposite Deb's, a thick hand, surprisingly pinkish; the fingers reminded me of uncooked sausages. You could fit two of Deb's into that hand. He started right in talking, but I couldn't hear anything he was saying. He was one of those body talkers, getting everything into the act: eyebrows rising and falling, blinking, legs in constant motion even when sitting, then every so often he'd shut both eyes and sort of scrunch up the middle of his face for a second; I guess you'd say it was a tic he had. Then he started drumming his sausages against the glass, but it just happened on its own, something he wasn't conscious of. I remember thinking the guy must burn off a load of calories just being awake. I heard Deb say my name, and he looked at me, nodding the whole time, little vibrating nods, almost like he was having some kind of attack. Then he gave me a wink, moved the phone away from his face, threw his hands to the sides of his head and mouthed an exaggerated *hello* as if he were a clown or in the middle of a mime routine. Deb leaned forward, laughing. She said the little show reminded her of something Carl did as a kid, and she started talking again. I wondered if it would be that easy for them to begin again after almost twenty years. If I didn't see my brother or sister for two decades, could we find those old connecting gestures and bonds as quickly as Deb and Carl seemed to? And if we could, wouldn't we be connecting with the person we remembered, rather than who that person had become?

I felt a bit like a third wheel just standing there. Carl was a question mark in more ways than one. I'd get my chance to talk to him sooner or later, but what did we really have to say to each other? It wasn't as if we could sit around with him for the whole day or have him over for the weekend. The guy was in jail. What could be accomplished realistically in a couple of minutes of talking on a phone? I was glad to be a nobody, sitting off to the side, and glad to see Deb so happy.

Deb looked up at the clock, then at me.

"Carl says they cut the phones off in six minutes, at four o'clock."

"Well you'd better keep talking then. Tell him we'll come back tomorrow."

I heard him saying her name a number of times through the receiver. When she turned back he was talking a hundred miles an hour, the goofy clown expression gone. A bit later she tugged my sleeve and said, "Lloyd Walker, remember that name." I would have written it down, but the guards had made us empty everything from our pockets when we came in. Carl kept on talking a streak, waving his free hand, scrunching his face in the middle, and the whole time all Deb said was, "Yeah, Okay, Right." Then the phone went dead, just like that. They nodded at each other, as if an agreement had been made, and we made our way to the door.

We got a room in a motel halfway between the jail and the downtown area. It turned out there was more to Carl's story than we knew. He had laid everything out for Deb in those last six minutes, when he realized the next day was Friday, the last business day of the week, and we would be back home in Canada on Sunday. He wanted us to see this Lloyd Walker fellow the next day. Walker was a lawyer Carl had heard about, and Carl apparently needed a lawyer in a big way, because in addition to the theft, he had also been charged with setting a cell block on fire while in jail. He had told Deb the legal assistance system was phony to the nines. The most anyone would do for him was argue for reduced time; nobody was interested in any real defense. It was all a racket he said, a legalized mafia. Some inmate had started a fire that cost the county a ton of dough, and even more embarrassment, and they couldn't find out who did it. So they shut the prisoners in their cells for a week, took away their smokes, purposely burned or undercooked their food, but no one came forward with any information. Now they needed a scapegoat, some guy who was in the area and who was basically defenseless, an easy target. Carl said they went after him because he had no money, no family or friends who would come to his rescue, and to top it off, after the apartment scene, the cops wanted to make sure they didn't have to put up with him for a long time. So now he was looking at three to five years in the big house, just for assuming some junk patio furniture had been left behind.

"Why didn't that Norma woman tell you all this?" I asked.

"Carl told her not to. He knows he should have, but when she found me he was afraid I wouldn't come if I knew everything."

"I wonder what else we don't know." I could picture him twitching, throwing his hands to his head, smiling.

"We just need to talk to a real lawyer."

"We?"

"It's just a...oh, what do they call it? Not an investigation. It's a...discovery, that's what he said, just a discovery. The lawyer meets with Carl, takes a look at the files, the charges, talks to the court people. That's all. He just wants to be treated fair."

"Who's paying for this discovery? Lawyers down here are worse than in Canada."

"It can't be too much. Just a discovery. What, three or four hours? How much can that cost?" She was already going through the phonebook.

"Well, at one hundred and fifty an hour, that's about two and a quarter, no, two-fifty an hour Canadian..."

"Carl said Walker sometimes takes on special cases, charges less. A kind of rebel. Look," she said, glancing up from the phonebook, her eyes reddening, "I don't want you to do this for Carl, but for me. Let's see what Walker has to say. I know what you're thinking about Carl, but I'm not prepared to go there yet, not this soon. He's my brother. He was left behind. It wasn't fair. Who knows what he's been through. I can't..."

The meeting with Lloyd Walker was sandwiched between his other commitments, and it was over in fifteen minutes. For two hundred and fifty U.S. he would let us know if Carl's story had any merit. It was a surprisingly reasonable fee. Walker was no-frills, a straight shooter, making no attempt to hold anything back. He told us what it might cost to defend Carl, if that was what was needed, and how unfairly people were often dealt with on the inside. But he also let Deb know that jail can make a child-murderer sound like a victim, that manipulation is one of the only games a prisoner has left, and he has nothing to lose by attempting to get anyone on the outside to fight for him. It was clear to me he wasn't passing judgment on Carl so much as reading the innocence and desperation so obvious in Deb. It was worth every cent to have someone else say exactly what she was not willing to hear from me.

Two more visits to the jail and the weekend finished on a whirlwind of hope: Carl would get his lawyer and Deb would never be brotherless again.

Six weeks and a little over three thousand dollars in legal fees later we were heading back to the States. Walker had used the word "expunged" in his last letter, which to me sounded like the legal system in Montana was prepared to suck it up, take its losses, so to speak. We looked up the word and were surprised to find out we had basically given Carl a new life, free of any dark past. It seemed Carl's story about the fire had some validity. He was, apparently, in the wrong place at the wrong time, and they needed to point a finger at someone; either that or they had nothing to make the charge stick. Once Walker had made it known Carl was not alone in the world, all the charges started being reduced or dropped. The value of the patio furniture was seriously lowered when Walker reminded the neighbour about a certain disagreement he and Carl had about an illegal smoking substance.

The only catch to this expunged business was they wanted Carl out of the state, or, "Better yet," as Walker had said on the phone, "why don't you give them some particulars about yourselves, get some professional people in your town to give you a reference, tell the authorities down here that you'll take him right out of the country. It wouldn't hurt. They like that kind of thing down here, passing trouble on to some other authority." So we went around town, getting a lawyer friend of my parents, our family doctor and Brian, my boss, to write letters about us being decent, law-abiding citizens. We didn't say anything to them about Carl being in jail, just that we were considering sponsoring his entrance into the country. The plan at the time was to give the Montana courts the most favourable impression possible, make them think Carl's reunion with his sister would change everything about the guy, including his permanent address. We weren't lying so much as letting them believe what they already wanted to. I suppose it sounded a lot like we were offering to rehabilitate him, and it worked. Truth was, the farthest ahead we saw was bringing Carl up to Canada to spend some time with Deb, get to know Brucie and find his bearings. We hadn't set a time limit, but in the back of my mind I had figured a few weeks of being together would be a good start for them.

The lot I had been looking at was out of the question now, what with all the lawyer's fees, but the whole thing made me feel pretty darn good all the same. Outside of marrying Deb and raising Brucie, I remember thinking it was as close as I'd ever been to feeling like I'd made a real impact in the world. It seemed a small price to pay for making Deb so happy and for giving Carl back his life.

Because of work, the return trip to bring him up to Canada had to take place on a weekend. We took Brucie this time and left on Friday evening, planning to drive well beyond midnight so we could get into the States before calling it a night. The usual questions at the border took on new meaning when we realized Carl would be with us when we came back the next day. We knew enough to keep everything simple, both of us saying we were Canadians and that we were going to visit her brother in Missoula, then wondering as we drove away if they had a computer with different information from our previous trip, when Deb claimed to have dual citizenship. And of course we weren't going to visit her brother, we were going to bring him back; so there'd be four of us, not three, back at the border the very next day. And what if they asked about criminal records, like they sometimes did? We didn't know *when* Carl's record would be erased, but it was unlikely they moved any faster in the States than they did in Canada. I knew they had a shared computer system at the border that tracked license plate numbers, but what else did they keep on file?

We decided on a basic in-and-out operation, both of us joking nervously about international incidents, spy rings, commandos, smugglers, putting a beret on Brucie and painting his face black. We studied a map and decided we'd re-enter through a different crossing, further west, drive right through the top of Idaho and then up from Washington. The trip would take longer, but at least we'd avoid being visually recognized by the same officers. I didn't think we were prepared to lie to get Carl into Canada, but it was clear the truth would do us no good at all.

So the next day we swooped into Missoula, loaded all of Carl's belongings, which amounted to two dufflebags, into the van, paid his motel bill, dropped off a final cheque at Walker's office and began to angle our way back to Canada. Carl had never been further north than Great Falls, and despite having lived twenty-eight years within hours of the border, he didn't appear to have spent a moment of his life wondering what might lay beyond the forty-ninth parallel. To Carl, Calgary may as well have been some kind of fish you trolled for in the North Atlantic, though he did seem vaguely aware of British Columbia having something to do with draft dodgers and dope farms.

We spent the next seven hours going west more than north, and often winding south for half an hour or more before finally arcing north or west again. All day long it was two or three steps forward followed by one backward step. And every hour Carl would make a big production out of rolling himself a smoke, beginning by clearing his throat, extending both arms toward the front of the van, then massaging the air with his fingers as if he were a magician about to perform a trick. He took great pleasure with these frequent displays, as did Brucie, who by the fourth or fifth smoke break was studying Carl's rolling skills with the precision of a scientist. So we kept having to pull off the road to accommodate a habit neither Deb nor I had much patience for, especially Deb, who saw almost any indulgence as the first step on the road to nowhere.

"When we get home," Deb told him on our first stop, "there's no smoking in the house, ever. Understand?"

"Yes, Sis. Ma'am. Sir."

Deb filled him in on Brucie being a gift we were lucky to have, that the boy meant she had been given a chance to make up for everything their mother had failed at so miserably. How we had tried for over a year to have a baby; the tests we both went through and finally finding out she had fibroids in her uterus. How the doctor said she'd never be able to have a baby, then the chances we took when she actually did get pregnant; her hysterectomy the following year. Carl did a lot of nodding as she spoke, though I suspected he had next to no idea of the inner workings of the female body. The story wasn't needed to get Carl involved with his new nephew; he already had Brucie going wild much of the time, what with his penchant for making faces and his inability to sit still for more than half a minute. At four and twenty-eight, they were a perfect match for each other. Before we had left Idaho, Carl had become Unkie Car to Brucie.

When we told him about the potential trouble at the border, he didn't seem concerned, adding that he was prepared to say or do whatever he had to in order to get into Canada. It wasn't a heavily weighted comment, especially given our precarious involvement. Then I told him customs officers are more like cops than K-Mart security guards. The difference between the two is that cops are supposed to serve and protect, but customs officers aren't much into the serving end of the business, that they often took the protect stuff pretty seriously and they had powers that would make the meanest street cop envious. By the time we approached the border crossing around midnight, we had organized a number of safe answers to every possible question we could think of. I had even gone so far as to give Carl about one hundred and fifty dollars to add to whatever money he already had, in case he had to prove he could finance his holiday. Regarding the criminal record question, if asked, we would answer individually, all of us saying no, and if Carl was caught, Deb and I would act as if we knew nothing about this area of his past. If we were going to run into trouble, Carl agreed he should be the one to take the heat.

Deb gave Carl a comb and told him to fix his hair. As we pulled in under the lights he pretended to have just woken up. I hoped Brucie being asleep in his carseat would help make us appear pretty harmless. The officer asked all the usual questions while he looked in my window, into the back, smiled at Brucie sawing logs, gave Carl a quick pass over.

"Do you have anything in the back to declare?"

"No," I said, almost whispering, making it as obvious as I dared to suggest that waking a four year old at this time of night would cause all hell to break loose. The officer walked around to the rear windows and shone a flashlight over the bed and around our bags on the floor. Ours wasn't one of those fancy minivans with lots of windows, but a cargo van that I got mostly for work. Except for the bed and a benchseat from an old school bus I'd bolted to the floor, it was usually full of tools. I looked back at Carl; it was the longest I'd ever seen him sit still, and he looked like he was about to crack into pieces with the effort. Deb's head was against the door now, her eyes closed like she was trying to catch a few winks, but I knew she had fallen into one of her instant trances again. In her mind she probably already had the four of us well into Canada, on some mountain pass, the moon's white light pouring over us. Her lips had just begun to curl upward when the officer reappeared, waving the flashlight to say we were free to go. No one had to lie or stretch the truth. For a mile or so we still held our breath, and we would have broken into a celebration at that point if Brucie hadn't been sound asleep.

There were still over four hours of driving ahead of us, but we were back in Canada, on our own turf. We were virtually alone on the highway. It was a perfect night, a scattering of big rolling clouds lit up by a near-full moon, the sky sinking deep and dark in between them, the air sharp with the chill of fall. At every summit we were met with a burst of light and clarity.

With some prodding from Deb, Carl sat between us on the floor and started telling us stories from his time in and out of the orphanage. He said he had a lot of respect for the nuns who ran the place, that they weren't mean and bitter old bags like people usually think. They always had at least one dog and one cat living with them, usually strays found in the winter. The year Deb left, when he was nine, he was fostered out to a man who had a fourteen-year-old retarded son. The man didn't want another child; he wanted someone for his son, Morris, to play with.

"Morris was an idiot," said Carl. "A big fucking idiot." I glanced at Deb, who had also reacted to his language, then at Brucie in the rear-view mirror. At least Carl had the sense to wait until Brucie was asleep. "Whenever his old man left the house, Morris would amuse himself by beating me on the head with a shoe, a leather one, must've been around size thirteen." He threw an arm over his head, let out a little hysterical laugh and hammered his fist down on his knee.

"How long did that last?" I asked.

"About four months." He was still acting out the scene, rolling his head around like he'd just had his brains squashed.

"Stop it," said Deb, giving him a light kick. He kept it up until she finally turned away.

"What else?" I asked.

He squinted, then, with a grand flourish, pulled the bag of tobacco from his shirt pocket and held it in the air between us, letting us know the next story was going to cost us.

"When I was eleven I moved in with Barb and Erik Helmsman. A real family. They were good people, older, maybe in their forties. Couldn't make their own kids, so they came shopping." He opened the pouch, took out the little packet of papers and peeled one off, every motion ending with some exaggerated gesture. "They did interviews before, you know: how I was doing in school, behaviour stuff, personal history. I'd been what you might call shortlisted a few times after escaping from the idiot's place, so I knew the game. They never liked finding out about Mom being such a wingnut, but the bit about being separated from Sis usually got them on my side right away. It was another foster thing, of course. No one wants to adopt anyone over three or four. Except for Sis, right? Erik was an outdoors man, into hunting, fishing. We got along pretty good, maybe too good as far as Barb was concerned. She was the stay-at-home type, really pretty, but nervous, edgy, especially at the end."

The cigarette was rolled now and he raised it to his mouth to lick, but stopped, as if having just realized something.

"I think she might've been the reason they couldn't have kids, and maybe she let it work on her too much. That's probably what made her nervous." He nodded in agreement with himself.

There was something on the road, far ahead; the high beams had just barely begun to capture it.

"I suppose they hoped I'd fill them out as a couple, a kind of do-or-die situation."

It looked like a cardboard carton, a big one, flattened, something that might have held a stove.

"If I had been a girl," Carl continued, "it might have worked, for Barb anyhow, but not with me and Erik heading into the bush every second weekend." He licked the paper and ran one of those pink fingers down the side of the cigarette.

The box was right in the middle of the road, but the highway was nice and wide, the shoulders paved; I figured I'd have no trouble getting around it.

"Course a lot of this didn't make much sense until I was older. They might've stayed together, who knows?" He placed the cigarette under his nose and inhaled a satisfying breath.

Deb gasped and pointed to the road.

We were almost on top of the box, but she didn't know I had been keeping my eye on it for almost a mile. Carl rose onto his knees to see what had gotten her attention. There was no traffic and I was just about to tell her to relax, that we had lots of room on either side of the road, when the box shook a bit to the left, then back toward our lane. We were no more than fifty feet away when I went for the brakes, realizing too late that the "box" was a deer lying on the road, struggling to get out of the path of the lights, and that if we hit it and crashed into the ditch or bush no one might find us until the next day. Then I changed my mind and took my foot off the brake and punched the gas, thinking that if we ended up hitting it, we'd be better off having as much force behind us as possible. We roared past, clutching the shoulder of the highway, missing it by inches, the deer raising its head on its long neck, staring straight into the high beams before collapsing back on the road. We came to a stop, then backed up several hundred feet and got out.

White moonlight spread across the highway, and the cold silence outside the van seemed to be magnified by the surrounding dark mountains. It was a doe, I knew that much because the top of her head was bare and smooth, but I had no idea how old or what kind of deer she was. She was attempting to crawl into the bush on the other side of the road, lifting herself on her front legs, dragging her damaged hind quarters across the pavement. Her front hooves were clawing and clacking against the road, sounding like stone-on-stone. Some vehicle just ahead of us had obviously hit her. There was a flash of light to my left as Carl lit his cigarette.

"Broken spine," he said, before sucking the smoke deep into his lungs, holding it there for a second, then exhaling. "The whole hind end smashed to shit." A wall of smoke floated in front of me. I could hear the frosted grass crunch under his feet as he disappeared into the ditch.

Deb was in a panic, yelling for me to do something, but all I could think of was the agony the deer must be in and that the only thing to do was find a way to end her suffering.

Carl called to me from the ditch. He had found a long piece of wood, which looked like an old fencepost, but he couldn't free it from the ground by himself. I knew what he was up to right away. The two of us heaved it free. It was a little over four feet long, about twice the thickness of a 2x4. He dragged it up to the road and went straight for the deer.

Brucie broke out crying and Deb, who was following right behind Carl despite her constant disgust of anything remotely violent, suddenly caught herself and turned to run back to the van.

Carl wasted no time. He had the post hoisted over his head by the time he reached the middle of the road. The deer had stopped struggling a few feet from where the ditch began. She was pointed away from us, her head held several feet above the ground as she stared into the bush. A stream of vapor jetted from her nose as each hot breath struck the cold air. I could hear the choking gargle of blood in her lungs, the fear in every breath. There was no sign she was aware of Carl behind her, even though I could clearly hear the grunt he made as he drove the post at the top of her skull. There was a resounding crack as wood impacted bone, followed by another crack, further off in the bush, as the sound bounced off an adjacent hillside. The deer's head dipped toward the road, then bobbed up again, swooning on the end of that long neck, then turning in the general direction of Carl. I could hear Carl's voice again, *Morris was a big fucking idiot*, and remembered him rolling his head as he sat between us in the van just a few minutes earlier. He lifted the post once more, and in one motion brought it down again, a glancing hit this time, off the back of the skull, most of the force landing on the neck. The post broke free of his grip and bounced into the ditch.

"Jesus-fucking-Christ," he yelled out, as he leaped down the incline, the same words ringing off the hillside a moment later.

Everything appeared to be going backwards. This last blow seemed to put the deer on full alert. Her front legs were surprisingly furious now, smashing down on the pavement with lethal force. I ran to the ditch and met Carl on his way up, dripping with sweat and muttering every curse imaginable, with the post slung over his shoulder.

"I'll get the son of a bitch this time," he said, stomping right past me.

He charged at the deer, screaming like a wildman as he swung the post. He wasn't just killing a deer. He was clubbing those cops and lawyers back in Missoula who wanted to send him to prison, and bashing the dopehead neighbour who owned the furniture. Or maybe he was venting his frustrations over being left behind in the orphanage, or against his mom for abandoning him, for killing herself. The immediate target was the deer's skull, but he was also swinging at something in his past that, perhaps, even he could not identify. This time it was a direct hit, except the impact snapped the post in two. Her hooves stopped again, but her neck somehow remained elevated. Carl looked at the stump in his hands, recognizing its uselessness. We both began searching the ditch for another post or log. Everything was either too small, too big, or rotten. I could still hear Brucie; he was screaming now, not just crying.

"There's nothing here," I yelled. "It's all crap."

"Here," cried Carl, and he held up a rock about the same size as his head.

"It's no good," I said. "You can't get that close. Those hooves could kill you."

But he was already climbing to the road.

"It's all there is."

Then Deb called out, "Carl, use this." There was a series of high-pitched clanging sounds above us, like someone had dropped a pipe on the pavement. We scrambled up to the road, both of us yelling, "Use what?" in unison as the clanging sounds echoed back.

"The tire iron. Use the tire iron." She was at the back of the van, pointing at the road between us. The back doors were open and I could see Brucie standing perfectly still on the bed.

Carl dropped the rock and started sweep-searching the pavement.

"There," she yelled. "Keep going. To the left."

He came back toward me, nodding and smiling and panting, the tire iron held out like a victory torch. "That's my Sis," he said as he passed me.

Deb shut the back of the van and was hurrying to the side door, wanting to make sure Brucie couldn't see the deer. I could see him through the back windows, still standing on the bed, his face almost pressed to the glass.

I turned just in time to see the L-shaped tire iron collide with the top of the deer's skull. Her head went straight to the ground this time and Carl let out a whoop. Then he bent forward and brought the iron down on her head again. There was a soft crunch and her body went into a sort of mild shaking fit—death tremors is what I think it's called. It was over in a matter of seconds. I looked back at the van; Brucie and Deb had disappeared but I could hear sobbing.

Carl surveyed the body from head to tail, then stood and walked toward me, already reaching into his shirt for a smoke. He was shaking his head in amused amazement, then chuckled as he pointed the tire iron at me.

"You ever see such a tough bugger? Christ, damn near killed me. Thought I was going to beat the motherfucker to the grave there for a while." He slapped me on the upper arm, dropping the tire iron next to his foot, and began rolling a smoke.

Deb called out from behind the van, her voice breaking apart, "Is it over?"

"You bet," replied Carl over his shoulder. "The tire iron, Sis, that's the tool all right." He nudged me with an elbow. "Have to remember that for next time, right brother?"

Brother? Apparently this primitive bloodbath had somehow brought the two of us together.

I told him we had better get the deer off the road before someone really did get killed. I meant to drag it into the ditch, let the coyotes and crows feast on it. But Carl had other plans. He said he didn't beat the living shit out of it just to put it out of its misery.

"Trust me," he said. "Chop off that one rear quarter where the car hit, and you still have a couple of hundred pounds left. That's a lot of deer-kebab."

I didn't know what they did in the States, but I told him it was illegal to keep it in Canada. He stepped into the middle of the highway, put his hand over his eyes like an Indian scout out of a cheap Hollywood movie, and pretended he was looking up and down the road. I knew what he was saying. I also knew if I let him go any further, he'd probably get down on all fours, put an ear to the ground and provide a running commentary about some eighteen-wheeler cresting a hill five miles behind us. I thought of the patio furniture sitting on his neighbour's lawn.

"Um, plenty good meat there," he said, pointing to the deer.

"Deb and I, we're not big meat eaters," I said. It was true. We had red meat only occasionally, about two or three times a month, mostly as a treat for me. Since getting married Deb had been trying to get me to swear off meat completely. For her, a diet based around grains and beans was a sign of moral maturity, proof that we were able to further distance ourselves from our savage ancestors.

"What do you mean you don't eat meat?" He seemed truly shocked. "Everyone eats meat."

"Besides," I said, "it's probably filled with adrenaline and tastes awful."

"Do you have any idea what they feed you in jail?" His head and face started into a round of familiar, aggravated twitches. "Three days ago I would've killed for a stinking slab of smashed venison."

I remember thinking that every one of those tiny ten-thousand-movements-a-day would require feeding. I thought of Deb trying to get him to chow-down on her bulgar salad, and her tofu, eggplant and brown rice casserole, or the unlikelihood of Deb putting up with the smell of fried meat filling the house. But he was a big man, no doubt with a big appetite, and we had already dropped a small fortune on him. The deer could save us more than a few dollars.

He said he would eat it even if it did stink, and that he had helped Erik Helmsman clean and carve up a moose, so we didn't have to worry about butchering.

In the end it was Deb who made the decision, giving in to Carl, going against what I knew she considered her better judgment, forgiving his lack of moral maturity, saying Carl could take it home if he had to, but she would have nothing to do with cooking it or cleaning up after. And she didn't want pieces of bloody meat laying around inside the refrigerator. She was dead beat at the time, just like me, and didn't have the energy to mount much of a defense.

So we moved all our bags up onto the bed in the back of the van, then heaped the deer onto the floor just behind the benchseat, the musky swamp smell seeming more the smell of death than anything living. Brucie spent the rest of the trip anchored to Deb's lap, refusing to sit in his car seat. All the way home he kept pointing to the mountain of brown hair on the floor and whispering, "Giraffe. Giraffe."

An hour back in Canada and there we were, the once decent law-abiding citizens with an ex-con alien and two hundred pounds of illegal roadkill.

When I came home from work on Monday I went straight to the shed in the backyard. Three large plastic bags were lying on the grass, each of them heavily weighted down, and all of them splattered with blood and clumps of spiked hair. When we had arrived home in the middle of the previous night, Carl and I had dragged the deer into the shed before going to bed. I told him the neighbours on both sides were friends of our landlord, and they kept a pretty close eye on the place. Whatever he had to do to the deer, he'd have to do it inside the shed and the door would have to be closed at all times. The hollowed out carcass was hanging in the middle of the shed, suspended from a yellow nylon rope that had been punched through two parallel holes in each rib cage. The legs and everything from the base of the neck up were missing, and there was a large mangled area, a crude hole where he had hacked away at the bottom of one side, no doubt where the car had hit the deer. I knew the carcass would have to hang for a week or so in the cool fall air before being cut up. The floor was littered with tools—handsaws, tin snips, side cutters, a hammer, screwdrivers, a crowbar, two of my prized carving chisels—all of them covered in the blood and guts that had already begun to dry and stick to the floor. The Makita circular saw I had recently bought was sitting right under what remained of the deer. I moved it out of the path of blood that had been dripping on it for who knew how long and looked to the shelf on my right. There sat my old beater circular saw, in plain view, not a spot of blood on it. I made a mental note to remember to get back the one hundred and fifty dollars I'd given him before crossing the border. I figured it would take a couple of hours to clean up the mess, and several years to forgive the idiot for what he had done to my tools. I picked up the chisels, unsuccessfully trying not to imagine what he must have done to them, set them on the workbench and headed for the house.

I could hear Brucie running to the door as I came in. I prepared for the customary greeting we had fashioned over the last year: he would wait at the top of the three steps going down to the landing, and when I was at the bottom of the stairs he would spread his arms as wide as he could and leap toward me. But he had barely stopped at the top of the stairs when Carl called for him, and the next second Brucie was running back to the living room.

"Hi," called Deb from the kitchen, her voice sounding surprisingly energetic considering what little sleep we'd all had. The house was filled with the smell of fresh bread and something with lots of garlic in it.

I heard a guitar being strummed a couple of times, then Carl's voice as he began to sing. By the time I was in the living room Brucie was standing and facing Carl, who had discovered Deb's old guitar in the basement. Both of them were singing a song Brucie had learned at playschool, the one about the wheels on the bus that go round and round. It was pretty clear Carl knew how to use a guitar, and Brucie was completely mesmerized, the picture of innocence. Carl looked up and gave me another one of his famous winks. Deb came around the corner, her lips creased into a smile. She was holding her shoulders as if to say, *What can I say?*; as if she knew all about my tools and the mess in the shed; as if she knew that somehow the Carl who had blundered once more had also found a way to allow us to forgive him again.

The rest of the week was an exercise in exhaustion: working the expected ten hours a day, plus overtime, then hauling myself home to supper, listening to Carl and Brucie's latest song, then showering and heading straight to bed. But going to bed turned into another kind of labour.

Carl's habits were the opposite of ours. When we went to bed, he would disappear into the makeshift room we'd set up for him in a corner of the bare cement basement. What we had put together for Carl in the basement was likely no improvement on his cell in Missoula: a mattress on an old 9x12 area rug, one of Brucie's dressers and two bed sheets hanging from the floor joists that did little more than offer the illusion of privacy. It was the best we could do seeing as we were renting a small, one-storey house from the post-war era, with two bedrooms on the main floor, both of them small. Once the house quieted down we could hear him playing guitar and singing beneath us; we could hear the click of the pull switch on his ceiling light; we could hear him pass gas and change positions on the bed; and we could hear him snore when he finally did go to sleep. He kept the volume down when he was singing, but I could hear enough to know when he was playing something I thought I recognized, but never enough to know the singers or the lyrics. They weren't the type of songs we would have chosen to listen to, but there was no escaping them now. And several times a night I would be awakened by footsteps on the stairs, the sound of the refrigerator opening, the toilet flushing or the click of the front door whenever he went for another smoke. And of course we knew that if we could hear him, then he could hear us. We were afraid to touch each other, so we didn't; we were afraid of making any kind of noise that could be misconstrued. We choreographed our movements, both of us changing positions at the same time to avoid any extended creaking of the bedsprings.

Yet somehow, despite the constant disruptions Carl brought upon us, Deb got up every morning bright and light-hearted, as if each day were a blessing. She happily threw herself into the role of the queen of all mothers, putting on a spread for every supper, fussing over Carl and Brucie. I always thought she had been born too late, that she would have been the ideal Mom in 1955. She was particularly taken with having a brother who was also a musician, especially since she always wanted to be one herself but had never gone beyond buying the guitar and taking a couple of complementary lessons. I could tell it was a confirmation of sorts for her, a powerful proof of their connectedness, to realize they both shared not only the desire to play music, but also the same instrument. Her smiles seemed to say that their shared roots were stronger than the two decades that had separated them. Apparently he hadn't had a guitar for over a year, and Deb said that aside from going out to smoke in the backyard and drinking twenty cups of coffee a day, he had spent most of that first week making up for lost time on the guitar. She had never seen anyone put so much time into something that she considered really just an amusement. And except for playschool, Brucie rarely left his side; seeing them together was like watching something out of the Pied Piper story.

She also said that when he did stop playing, he'd just appear out of nowhere, leaping into the kitchen or living room or bedroom, surprising her with one of his theatrical entrances, moving every which way, squinting and twitching, asking, "How ya doing?" or "What ya doing?" or "What ya making?" Then he'd start wrestling with Brucie or chasing him down the hall and around the furniture. The boy would be screaming with joy, at least she supposed it was joy, though the pitch and amplitude of his scream was something she had never heard from him before, a noise that only Carl could bring out of him, and one that might have otherwise raised alarm. The whole house would vibrate from their running. It bothered Deb that Carl didn't seem to know the difference between fun and hysteria, and more often than not he wouldn't stop until Brucie had crashed into a wall or a chair or slipped and hit his head on the kitchen floor. Then Brucie would start crying and Carl would try to pick him up, but the boy would start kicking and screaming all the more because he didn't want "Unkie Car," he wanted his mom. It would take Deb fifteen minutes to get him settled down, and all the while Carl would sit on the couch, looking long-faced and guilty, as if it were a requirement of his penitence that he stay in view. When he'd had enough of that he'd go outside to smoke and look at the carcass in the shed. And before the day was over they'd both be at it again.

After supper on Friday Carl announced he had a plan.

"That's great," I said. All week I had avoided asking him what he was going to do to get his life back in order. Deb leaned forward and nodded enthusiastically.

"I figure it's time to check out this town," he said. "What d'ya say, brother? How about you show me some of that Canadian night life. Head off to the local igloo for a few? What d'ya say?"

Despite finding Deb's guitar in the basement and almost every valuable tool I had in the shed, he apparently hadn't noticed there was absolutely no evidence to suggest we were drinkers. I sometimes had a glass of wine or a beer on special ocassions, but I hadn't been in a bar since before Brucie was born, and Deb hadn't finished a beer by herself in the whole time I had known her. She had always been a prudent social drinker, and as far as she was concerned, a bar was where people like her mother hung out, people with trash lives who chose alcohol over being responsible, and she'd made a point of having absolutely no connection to them.

Deb fell back in her chair and sighed; it was the first gesture of exasperation she had expressed in front of Carl. Her lips parted in an enormous yawn. I could feel it spreading toward me across the kitchen table. It was obvious both of us would be lucky to stay awake long enough to get Brucie in bed. But Carl didn't see our exhaustion; he didn't see the meaning behind Deb sagging back into her chair. Carl had a plan and that's all that mattered.

He launched into one of his energetic head-nodding routines when I told him I had a better plan.

"I was talking to Brian at work today," I began. "He said he could use someone for a couple of days next week." Now it was Carl's turn to show disappointment. His head was perfectly still. I could tell he had a pretty good idea where I was going. "It wouldn't be much. You won't need any tools. The site is getting pretty cluttered and we'll be starting on the second floor by Tuesday, so there's a ton of material to haul upstairs. Lots of odds and ends to stack and load into the dumpsters."

He didn't appear overly eager at the prospect of work, but he didn't seem revolted either. He was obviously weighing the pros and cons, but against what agenda, I had no idea.

"It'll be a cash deal. Nothing big, but you should come out around sixty bucks a day."

"Sixty bucks, huh?" he said. "How many days?"

"It's up to Brian. It's a big job though. Two stories, 1,800 square feet, lots of gables. We're going all the way to lock up. You ever work on construction?"

"Sold cars, mostly," he said. "Lots of them. I could sell a car to a blind man. If you had two nickels to rub together, I could sell you a car."

"Well you can't do that here. You're in Canada, remember? On holidays, right? But Brian will pay cash."

Two hours later Deb and I were in bed, listening to him picking on the guitar and singing in the basement while we fell asleep. Any talk about his plan for the night had died when I mentioned getting him a job. But we were wrong, of course; we were always wrong when it came to Carl.

The next thing I knew, Deb had thrown off the covers and the bed was rocking. The room was still dark and there was no sign of light outside the window. She was already on her feet. There was a smell in the room.

"What's going on?" The clock read 4:33 in the morning. "What's that smell?"

"The kitchen," she said, as if that was all the information a man needed at this time of night.

I stood up as she opened the door; the smell was instantly stronger. Lights were on in the front of the house and I could hear noise in the kitchen. Deb went back to the closet for her robe.

When we entered the kitchen he was facing the stove, his back to us. A layer of smoke hung over his head. He swayed drunkenly back and forth, singing to himself as he stabbed a fork at something in the frying pan. Then it hit me: the bar, the deer—two of Carl's plans. He turned to the counter, a piece of sizzling meat the size of his hand impaled on the end of the fork. He was trying to figure out what to place it on, what cupboard the plates were in, when he noticed us.

"Hey! My favourite Sis and Bro!" He took an involuntary step backward, belched, then steadied himself by grabbing the counter with his free hand. "I met some Can-a-di-ans tonight," he said. "You people are all right." He looked at the meat on the fork for a second, as if trying to remember what it was, and what he was supposed to do with it.

Deb had already turned on the fan over the stove. "Do you know what time it is?" she asked. Now she was heading to open the kitchen window. "Are you some kind of animal? You can't sleep at night like real people?"

Grease was dripping off the meat and onto the floor, but Carl was oblivious. I took a plate from the cupboard and placed it on the counter. He assumed I was helping him and gave me what he could manage of one of his usual winks, then opened the cutlery drawer and pulled out a knife.

"You can't do this anymore," I said.

"Do what?" he asked, looking up from the plate. "I can't eat anymore?"

"You can't keep us up all night," said Deb. "You can't wander around all night, cooking, going to the bathroom, going in and out of the house every half hour, playing that guitar."

I told him we hadn't had a decent night's sleep since he arrived, that we were worn raw and he'd have to start thinking beyond himself. It was a strange feeling talking to someone his age as though he were a kid.

"You need structure," said Deb, her voice building in volume. "You've got too much time on your hands. Pull yourself together, for God's sake. Be responsible. Do you want to end up like Mom? You're headed in the right direction, you know. Do you want to end up dead in the gutter? Well congratulations, you're on the right path!"

I wasn't looking at anything in particular, but something on the inside of his left arm, below the elbow, caught my attention. It was a sort of bubbled pattern on the skin. Then I realized it was the first time I had seen him wearing a T-shirt. I wanted to grab his arm, turn it to the light and say, *What's this?* There were too many surprises. Too much we didn't know.

"I just went out for a few—"

"I'm not talking about tonight. I'm talking about your life."

Deb was already trembling and raking her fingers through her hair. There was no telling what she'd do if I put him on the spot about the marks on his arm.

"Listen," I said. "Nothing is going to get settled tonight. Carl, go to bed." He raised his knife as if to punctuate a point that hadn't yet made the trip from his brain to his mouth.

"Carl," I repeated, "go to bed. Take your meat if you want, but go to bed." He nodded once, as if what I had said was all he needed to hear, and staggered toward the stairs.

"And don't touch that guitar," said Deb, following right behind him, a full eight inches shorter, a hundred pounds lighter, her finger pointed at the back of his head. She stopped at the top of the stairs as he continued down. "You hear me? Not one bloody note."

I told her to settle down, that she was going to wake Brucie. After a brief protest she went back to bed, while I stayed behind to wash the dishes and try to get rid of the smell of fried meat in the air. It was after five in the morning when I got back into bed. Deb was lying on her back like a corpse, arms crossed over her chest, staring at the ceiling.

"Get some sleep," I said.

"Sleep? Yeah, right."

"Brucie's going to be up in a couple of hours."

"We'll send him down to the basement, see how his Unkie Car likes that."

"Why don't you do your thinking thing?"

"My thinking what?"

"You know, what you always do when you get upset."

She thought about what I had said for a few seconds, as if she was considering my advice, then rolled her back to me and said, "Why don't you just shut up."

I decided right then to not tell her about what I saw on his arm.

The next day Carl bent over backward to make up for what he'd done. He forced himself out of bed shortly after we had to get up with Brucie. After breakfast he took charge of the kitchen clean up. By ten he was in the shed carving up the deer, this time with the proper tools. In the afternoon he took Brucie to the playground down the street so Deb and I could steal a nap. And all day he stayed clear of the guitar.

On the evening news I found out there had been a fire the previous night near the downtown area. A two-storey building next to the tracks had been gutted, but no one had been hurt. They were pretty sure it had been set deliberately. I called Deb to come look at the television.

"Isn't that the building that church group held their meetings in?"

At the time we were thinking about joining a religion. Brucie was getting to the age where we felt he needed the right influences and codes to live by. We had looked around town and read some books from the library on faiths that were a little off-centre, but had strong family values. Deb squinted at the video footage on the television; there was smoke and flames everywhere.

"They're not a church group," she said. "They're not even Christian."

"They're not the aura-massaging bunch are they?" She gave me enough of a glance to let me know my little dig had been registered.

"It's a multi-faith thing," she said. "Remember? Christians. Jews. Hindus. Blacks. Natives. That's why we wanted to check it out."

She had refused to have anything to do with any religion that ranted on about original sin and hell and damnation, or the seed of Satan, or how we are all cursed for something that supposedly happened long before we were even born. Old-world religion, she called it, tales from the crypt. She said Brucie didn't need to hear about that stuff, and I agreed.

"Well," I said, "it doesn't look like there's much to check out anymore."

By nine o'clock the house was stone silent, just like it always had been before Carl had arrived. No guitar playing and singing beneath us. No one walking around opening doors. It was like we had reclaimed our lives.

On Sunday Carl was put to work rigging up a homemade barbecue in the garden, using some rocks and an old oven grill the landlord had left in the shed. I had a pile of lumber scraps we could burn. He licked his lips and got right down to business. I picked out a couple of deer steaks for the two of us, big ones like the one Carl had fried up, and Deb wrapped some potatoes and vegetables in foil and opened a package of tofu hot dogs for Brucie and herself. I even made a trip for a six-pack of beer. I saw the whole afternoon as a move on our part to show Carl we could bend, and that people didn't have to go as far as he did just to have a little fun.

I kept a close eye on him all weekend, watching to see if there was anything about his behaviour that explained what I had seen on his arm. I had no idea what to look for, but I thought there might be a clue in the wild energy Deb spoke of when he played with Brucie; and I had no idea what he might have been doing in the basement every night. But he seemed completely normal, the perfect brother-in-law.

In the end it was a good day, maybe the best day we had with him. Carl and I had our meat ration, the house didn't fill with the smell of fried fat, and Deb, who had not only finished a beer but had actually cracked open a second one, started apologizing and crying over what she had said about Carl heading for the gutter and following in their mother's footsteps. Carl shook it off by saying he had a habit of doing the wrong thing at the wrong time, saying the wrong thing, being in the wrong place—just plain being wrong most of his life— and that he was used to getting an earful from just about everyone. He explained that he had tried to figure out how he got this way, but the problem was he couldn't remember ever being any different. The whole story was laid out like a long and never-ending joke about his life: their crazy mother, being abandoned, the orphanage. He punctuated everything he said with all his now familiar expressions, self-depreciating jabs and accompanying physical antics, which would continue as long as they made somebody laugh, even if it was only a four year old. We drank our beer; we threw more wood on the fire. We let him talk and we even let him make us laugh at him. And yes, without actually discussing it, we forgave him again.

Brian wasted no time the next morning. He gave Carl a pair of gloves, pointed to the wheelbarrow and told him to toss every scrap of wood that was less than four feet long into the dumpster. Carl set off like a man on a mission: no wisecracks, no performances; a single nod and he was gone. There was nothing casual about the way he moved around the site; the day would be a long one, but he showed no sense of pacing himself. After coffee break he set to work organizing the longer scraps into separate stacks according to dimension and length. By the afternoon all the guys were calling on him whenever they needed an extra hand to brace or plumb a wall. When they wanted a piece of lumber from one of his piles, they'd call out what they needed: "Carl, buddy, 16-inch 2x6," "Carl, 34-inch 2x8." Carl would stop whatever he was doing and hurry over to the stacks, then study them for a few seconds until he isolated the 2x8s from the 2x6s and 2x10s. I had the impression this was the first time he noticed a 2x4 was only one of many different sizes of lumber, but by the end of the day he could tell the difference from ten feet away.

The next day he tried to open up a bit, testing a few of the guys who called out for a piece of lumber by doing a kind of monkey imitation, swinging between the stud walls or around corners, then tossing it to them. But it didn't work; no one gave him the laugh he needed to carve a space for himself. He'd have to compete on their turf and on their conditions. He started repeating whatever numbers they called out to him, calling them right back, like an echo. As the morning wore on I could hear a mocking edge in his voice whenever he repeated the numbers. It was as though Carl had imagined the guys were intentionally ridiculing him for not knowing the difference between a joist and a cripple and a header, or a spiral or galvanized nail. He assumed what they were really doing was treating him like a teenager on his first job, a twenty-seven-year-old gopher. They weren't poking fun at him so much as having fun with him; but Carl couldn't separate the difference between the two, probably because it was true: he really didn't seem to know much of anything worth knowing, and, in fact, he was more of a kid than he cared to admit.

After the truck dropped a load of lumber at the edge of the lot, he spent the rest of the day hauling what we needed for the second storey into the main floor of the house. It was the same grunt work I had to do fifteen years earlier, when I first started this job. Donkey work was where everyone started, and you were supposed to hate it. But Carl turned it into something else altogether. I guess he was trying to win some ground for himself to compensate for being in an environment where his usual strategies had no chance of gaining a toehold. You see the same muscle-bound mentality in teenage boys when they realize it's a lot easier to prove their worth with their bodies than with their brains. There was a difference with Carl, though, because he was an adult, not a kid; an adult who had mastered certain techniques and strategies that a teenager wouldn't have a clue of. A grunting teenager exploited his brawn because he had nothing else to exploit—except for a lot of bad movies and fantasies about various parts of the female body, a teenage boy's brain was largely empty. But Carl's brain wasn't empty: he could sell a car to a blind man; or turn a stranger like Norma into a private detective; for all I knew he could change colour and disappear in a ball of smoke. But not here, where the jargon was owned by others, where there was no stage, where everyone was always too busy to be his audience.

So he became a maniacal grunt staggering across the lot, hauling four or five 2x6s at a time when three would be plenty and two would be the norm; or hoisting two sheets of half-inch plywood against his shoulder when one was already difficult, occasionally missing the opening of the doorway because he couldn't see clearly, and ramming the wall, the whole side of the house shaking and terrifying everyone on the second floor. If the guys had been pulling his chain just a little in the past, they hadn't actually intended to get him worked up, but they upped the ante after the second time Carl rammed the wall. It could have been Carl's way of making sure he didn't have to come back the next day, or any other day, but every time the wall shook and the yelling started, he'd just continue on as if he were deaf. Mixed in with all of this I suppose he was punishing himself for not being able to fit into a normal adult working world. I felt sorry for him not having had the proper people around to teach him while he was growing up, and I felt sorry for him not being able to see the truth about himself, to see that no one can do a song-and-dance to get through life.

Brian paid Carl and let me know, in a kindly way, that he wouldn't need him anymore. Carl hadn't really done anything wrong, it was more a matter of not having done enough right.

On Friday I came home to find the house bursting with noise. There was some kind of machinery running in the bedroom, Brucie was charging up and down the hall, and above everything I could hear Deb and Carl laughing. I followed the noise to find the two of them in Brucie's room. Carl had the hose of a vacuum cleaner stuffed into a large plastic garbage bag; there was something bulky in the bag, but it was quickly shrinking smaller and smaller. It looked like they were shrink-wrapping something, and the smaller it got, the harder the two of them laughed. I looked at the machine again, thinking she must have decided to rent it to clean the rugs and furniture, but it wasn't at all like the big, boxy, four-wheeled machines we had used in the past. By the time Deb turned off the machine the bag and its contents could have easily fit into a breadbox.

Carl pulled out the hose, twisted off the bag and handed it to me.

"Isn't that amazing?" said Deb.

"What is it?" I asked.

"Brucie's quilt."

I opened the bag and saw the familiar pattern of cartoon characters.

"It's just been dry cleaned," said Carl. He pointed to a box on the floor that appeared to contain some kind of powdered cleaning chemical.

"It does pillows, too," added Deb.

"And shampoos carpets and upholstery."

I was starting to get a bad feeling.

"Dirt *and* liquids."

"It's a hair dryer."

"And a leaf blower."

"The motor is guaranteed for life."

They were having a great time, too much of a great time. It was like they were both infected by the same bug.

"Don't tell me you bought this."

"Well, actually," said Deb, "Carl bought it, sort of."

He was sitting on Brucie's bed, all smiles.

"Sort of? I need more than sort of."

"He put one hundred dollars down. In cash."

"A hundred?"

"And he beat the guy down four hundred more. So it's almost like he chipped in five hundred."

She said "chipped in,"so I knew there was more to come. Carl looked like he was about to give himself a medal.

"We already have a vacuum," I said.

"Not like this one," said Carl.

"Yeah? Well I also have a van, but it's not a Mercedes. What's the bottom line here?"

"Man, oh man," said Carl. "The bottom line is Sis got a hell of a vacuum cleaner."

"Forty-five dollars a month," said Deb.

"For how long?"

She said she was thinking of babysitting a kid or two for a couple days a week. I repeated my question.

"Thirty months," she said, finally.

"But there's no interest," said Carl. "I made sure of that. Show him the paper."

I was doing some crude math in my head. Apparently Carl had convinced Deb to unload around fourteen hundred dollars on a stupid vacuum cleaner. Everything was going the wrong way: Deb was supposed to be teaching Carl how to be responsible. Then I remembered the one hundred and fifty he never tried to give back to me, and the three grand for the lawyer, and close to another grand in gas and motels and phone calls. The total was something like six thousand dollars, enough money to frame and sheath a modest bungalow, and there he was, acting like he'd just saved me a ton of dough. I knew Brian paid him at least one hundred dollars.

"How much money do you have?" I asked. I did and I didn't know where I was going with this question. I was looking for a hole.

"What? On me?"

"No," I said. "How much do you have in total. In your pocket. In a bank. Stuffed in a sock."

He struck what he probably considered to be a thoughtful pose as he looked at the ceiling.

"Less than a thousand?"

One of his eyes twitched and he nodded.

"Less than five hundred?"

"About sixty-five bucks."

"That's it? Sixty-five dollars?"

"Pretty much," he said. "But I've lived on less." He made it sound like something to be proud of.

"I'm sure you have, but at whose expense?"

"He just wanted to help out," said Deb.

"You can have it all, right now, if you want." He started to dig those puffy fingers into his pocket. "It's just money, though the stuff you have up here is pretty funny looking. From what I hear, they're still making more of it everyday."

"*Your* money might be *just money*. But mine is mine."

"I wanted the vacuum in the first place," she said. "The old one was used when we got it. It could die any day. We'll never need another one."

His hand was still in his pocket when I left the room, and Deb had again launched into her promise to find some kids to babysit.

We planned to go to a wedding in Salmon Arm on the next Saturday, which was only a little over an hour's drive away. It was going to be an evening ceremony and Carl had somehow gotten Deb to agree to leave Brucie with him so we could stay over instead of coming home that night. She had never left him with anyone but my folks, and all week we had gone back and forth on the idea, finally deciding that, aside from Carl's igloo night, he hadn't really done anything serious enough to let us believe Brucie wouldn't be taken care of. His moodiness at work really had nothing to do with trusting him, and Deb was just as much at fault about the vacuum business as he was. After a whole week of watching him, I had found nothing about his behaviour to suggest the marks on his arm were anything other than blemishes, or maybe a burn from when he was a kid. I had already begun to convince myself that perhaps I hadn't really seen what I think I saw. Besides, we calculated we'd be gone less than twenty hours and Brucie would be sleeping for a third of the time. I had to admit that the prospect of an evening alone with Deb, without Carl lying beneath us, seemed too good to be true. Deb, of course, had laid down all the rules in black and white: no going out, no drinking, no smoking in the house, no sugar for Brucie, no screaming and chasing him around the house, and Carl could expect us to call home at least a couple of times during the evening.

We left mid-morning and everything went according to plan: Carl answered the phone every time we called; there were no strange noises in the background suggesting Brucie was upset; and around midnight, when Deb last called, she had gotten Carl out of bed. When we arrived home around noon the next day, Carl and Brucie were in the backyard getting ready to light another fire in the barbecue. There was a plate on a lawn chair with two pieces of meat on it: a large one and another smaller one that was obviously for Brucie. When Deb saw the plate she started to say something, then checked herself, no doubt thinking it wasn't that big a deal, it was just a little bit of meat. It wasn't as if Carl had turned Brucie into some kind of blood thirsty savage. That night Deb suggested I get permission from the landlord to put in a proper bedroom in the basement, nothing elaborate, but a room with real walls and a door, something Carl could call his own. I didn't say no.

On Tuesday night Brucie was in the living room, singing to himself and doing a little dance just before bedtime. I could hear Carl on the guitar in the basement, and Deb was in the kitchen. I wasn't paying any particular attention until Brucie sang something that sounded like it had the word "bitch" in it. When I looked up, he was standing near the entrance to the kitchen, with his legs spread apart and both his hands were on his crotch. To top it all, he was moving his hips in a circular motion. It wasn't the kind of show kids do when they know the world has cast a light on them; he was just being a kid, in his own world, nothing else. He was singing to himself, just as he always had, but this time it wasn't a song from playschool. *I'm a fox, I'm a bitch, and I wanna scratch my itch.* The words were clearly formed; he even had the accents in the right place. When he repeated the same line over, Deb appeared in the doorway behind him, her face marked with disbelief. We let him go through the song once more, mostly because neither one of us were prepared to admit what we had just heard. *I'm a fox, I'm a bitch, and I wanna scratch my itch.*

"Brucie?"

He stopped wiggling and looked at me.

"Where did you learn that song?"

"It's what Leslie did," he said.

"Who's Leslie?"

"Carl's friend from babysitting."

It was everything we didn't want to hear.

"Is that her dance?" asked Deb.

Brucie nodded and started to sing again.

I needed to find out more. I was tired of everything we had forgiven him for, everything we were too stupid to see.

"Brucie?...Brucie? Where did she do her dance?"

He pointed to the middle of the living room.

"And where were you when Leslie was dancing?"

He pointed to the far end of the couch.

"Did she have her clothes on?"

Deb gestured, as if to stop me from going too far, but then she held back.

Brucie said, "A little bit."

I heard Deb gasp, but I avoided looking at her. I could have stopped right there, but I needed to go as far as possible. I could tell Brucie wasn't going to follow my line of questioning much longer. I had to take a chance.

"Brucie, what did Unkie Car and Leslie do after the dance?"

A desperate gulping sound escaped from Deb's mouth.

"Horsey," said Brucie, then he turned to look where the strange noise had come from. I knew I had lost him now.

Horsey? I repeated the word to myself, wondering if I had heard correctly, or whether Brucie was even thinking about Carl when he said it.

Deb picked up Brucie, her arms locked over him as she pressed his body against her chest. She stared at me for a second, a scathing dry-eyed glare I had never seen before. I knew I had crossed the line with the last question. Then she very carefully mouthed the word "horsey," and a moment later she added the word "ride."

I mouthed the words back, questioningly: *Horsey ride?* And then it struck me. Deb's expression never wavered, but she nodded once when she saw I had figured out what she meant, then she carried Brucied down the hall to get him ready for bed.

We waited for Brucie to go to sleep before going down to confront Carl. We told him he had crossed us too often and we couldn't trust him anymore. He tried to deny everything, or at least make it seem a lot more innocent than the picture Brucie had given us: he and this Leslie were just goofing around, wrestling and laughing. He said Brucie was sound asleep on the couch; he must have woken up. Deb was livid.

"We're not buying it, Carl," she said. "None of it."

He threw his arms up in a gesture of disbelief, trying to make it seem like a crazy and hilarious mistake.

"We got you out of jail!" she said. "We gave you your life back!"

He just stood there, as if speechless in the face of such bizarre accusations. As though he thought there still might be a way out.

"It's not going to work," I said.

He finally dropped his arms and stared at the cement floor.

"Yeah, I know," he said. "It never does. I always fuck up." He looked at Deb like a dog that had just been beaten and left out in the rain. "Must be in my genes."

It sounded like he had at last admitted defeat, but he had really moved to another pattern, the "stupid me" routine, the "pity the poor orphan" scenario that must have worked for him countless times in his past. He was changing colours right in front of us, and I could see it clearly now.

"You have to leave," said Deb, moving toward the stairs, refusing to look at him altogether, as if she too saw right through him. "We'll figure something out tomorrow. But you can't stay any longer."

Then we left him standing alone and squinting under the ceiling light.

Late in the night I heard the familiar click of the door that signalled he had gone out for a smoke. But when we got up in the morning he was gone.

At work that morning I found out someone had lit a fire at the back of the house we were building. A neighbour saw the flames and the fire department arrived before it had done too much damage. The cops didn't think it had anything to do with the fire downtown, which they were now certain had been lit on purpose. I thought about Carl and the jail fire, how the downtown fire was lit when he could have been out of the house, even if we didn't know it, and now this one the morning after he disappeared. According to the cops, this last fire had all the makings of a kid's prank, but that didn't make me feel any better. Then one of the guys said that on his way to work he saw someone who looked a lot like Carl hitchhiking on the highway south of town. For a second I thought about jumping in the van to see if he was still there, but I had learned enough about him already.

I remember thinking about Norma back in Montana and that Carl could be headed her way, and maybe Deb should warn her.

Deb wouldn't talk about Carl after he left, even when Brucie kept asking where he was. Something in her had been taken away by her brother, or maybe something had been made obvious. Too obvious. For years now there's been an unwritten law in the house to never bring up his name. Except one night about five years ago, when Brucie was home alone, Carl called out of the blue from California. The boy knew he had an uncle in the States, that he had met him when he was four, but he had no memory at all of ever having met Carl. "Unkie Car" meant nothing to him. Absolutely nothing. And they talked for over half-an-hour, the two of them. Carl then thirty-five, Brucie twelve. Brucie told us Carl had just bought himself a 1966 Corvette, and he told Brucie it was a guaranteed babe machine. He wanted to know how many girlfriends Brucie had and what kind of music he listened to, and if he had learned to play his mom's guitar because it was a great way to attract girls. Brucie thought Carl was pretty cool, and California was cool, and some day he thought he would take a trip down there and have his uncle show him around. And when he was ready to buy his first car, he was going to go down for sure because Carl said he'd make sure Brucie got something that would do a lot more than just get him around town. He promised to roll out the carpet for the boy when he came.

Deb didn't want to hear any of it, but she listened to Brucie's story, then told him, without emotion or explanation, that Carl was nothing but trouble and he'd be doing himself a favour by staying clear of his uncle.

Brucie changed his name to Bruce around the time we last heard from Carl, and two years ago the boy got it in his head that everyone had to call him Bru. To be perfectly honest, we don't much care for the way the kid is turning out. He's become one of those surly types, failing at school, hanging around street corners all night, a different girlfriend every week, in trouble with the law. It's the hardest thing to end up with a kid you know won't amount to anything. You'd never know it to look at him, but his mother and I went out of our way to raise him right.

I rarely see the kid now that the economy around here has been beaten to death, what with the Americans raising tariffs on lumber, mills shutting down or running at half speed and copper prices taking a dive. I've been working out in Alberta for the past while, building ski resorts for the rich and famous. Deb's taken the brunt of dealing with the kid, but she's pretty well given up on him. She says there's no use fighting history. She works as a clerk in a drugstore down the street from the house we rent. In the evenings she takes classes in aura massage and aroma therapy, and last year she paid several hundred dollars for some sacred word that was supposed to rejuvenate all aspects of her life. She has a group of female friends who get together on weekends to practice ear candling and aligning the magnetic poles of their bodies. As far as I can tell, it's an enterprise that leaves her in a permanent state of exhaustion.

Nothing. That's what it all seems to come down to.

I know it's crazy, but it's like the seed of her mother was always there, in Deb, in Brucie. All it needed was a little nudge, a little reminder at just the right time. That's what they say about weeds, that the seeds can lie dormant in the ground for decades, waiting for some disturbance at the right time, the right season, a certain amount of rain.

I don't wish Carl any harm, but after everything that's happened since he came into our lives, I can't find it in me to wish him any good, either. As for Deb, she might hate Carl, but I suspect it's a matter of not being able to forgive him, but not for abusing the freedom we gave him; not even for what he did on that last weekend. My guess is Deb can't forgive him for making whatever happened in the past seem more permanent than anything she could do in the present. It's like he showed up only long enough to take away her future, and who could forgive anyone for doing that?

BOYS AND ARROWS

Without knowing it, we had somehow gotten older. Playing with stick rifles, drawing for teams and hiding in the trees behind my house was swept aside; it had become impossible to keep pretending. Our new game was never given a name, but the rules were simple. We used a bow and an arrow with a blunt lead weight on the tip. We would stand in a tight circle, out in the open field, five or six of us, no teams. We took turns launching the arrow into the air straight above us. With a twenty pound bow the arrow would just stay in sight, all of us watching as it made a lazy, innocent turn above our heads. At that moment we all stopped looking at the arrow and focused on each other, searching for signs of weakness, while somewhere above, gaining speed, a narrow shaft of terror headed our way.

With the plunging arrow the customary murmur would begin: *Whooo!* At first it was controlled and steady, but it quickly increased in intensity, rising in tone as if matching the acceleration of the arrow. The sound of fear gathered in our throats, growing louder and louder the longer we remained still, becoming a blinding noise that screened out all thoughts, except that of the descending arrow. Eyes and mouths took over more and more of each boy's face.

When someone finally allowed his fear, or common sense, to govern his actions, the established way of announcing it was to scream *Whaaa!* and run like hell. At that moment the rest of us would follow. Six boys tearing off in all directions; one thin arrow bearing down on them. Madness followed by the chaos of bodies stumbling over each other; hands and arms wrapped over heads, no one daring to look up.

The arrow would often strike within a foot or two of the circle, occasionally a bull's eye. But most of the time it would plunge to earth fifteen, twenty, or even thirty feet outside the perimeter. If the wind was blowing it didn't take long for everyone to realize the safest place to run was up-wind, causing a mad scramble in one direction. But on a calm day there was only one thing to do: run fast and keep running.

After the routine was established, and there had been no loss of life, two additional changes were made: a thirty-pound bow replaced the twenty-pound one; and a short time later someone arrived with a real arrow, razor-edged hunting tip included. The difference between the old bow and the thirty-pounder was substantial. When the arrow was shot from the more powerful bow, it completely disappeared into the sky, making its slow-motion turn where none of our straining eyes could see it. Furthermore, we could never be sure of the length of time each shot would require before it slashed to the ground— each pull on the bow was unique, each boy having more or less strength. The sky simply swallowed the now very lethal arrow, leaving no clue of its general direction.

Ben hadn't been around while we worked our way through the initial phase of the game—another one of his mysterious disappearances. When he finally showed up he took one look at the hunting arrow, smacked a fist into his palm and hollered, "Play ball!"

I was standing across from him as the arrow disappeared in the blue air.

"Whooo!"

When I looked back down to the group I got the feeling Ben hadn't been watching the arrow at all. He was staring straight at me, but not really looking at me so much as looking through me. It was like something was going on right behind me and he was able to see it even though I was in the way. He didn't even blink. And then someone broke away from the circle.

"Whaaa!"

From the very beginning the game had nothing to do with winning anything. There was no reason for anyone to either stay in the circle or be the last one to run to safety. It was possible to be a loser, but you could never be the winner. All of this seemed so obvious that I was sure no one thought there was a reason to even discuss it. In my desperate attempt to get to safety I tripped and fell about twenty feet from the circle. As I scrambled to my feet I noticed Ben. He hadn't moved at all; in fact, he still had the same blank expression on his face, like he was in a trance.

"Ben!" I yelled, trying to wake him up. His eyes were wide open, but they weren't moving. The arrow would land any moment now. I stepped toward him and started waving my arms. "Ben! Run! Come on!"

And then I heard it, slashing through the air to my left, so close I heard the feathers whipping back and forth. I looked down and saw it had knifed into the ground not more than two inches from my left foot. The shaft was still quivering. Everything started draining away and the ground came rushing toward me.

Faces. A circle of them hovering above me.

"You all right, Matt?"

I sat up.

"Yeah. Sure." It was true. I felt great. I couldn't stop smiling.

Everything seemed funny, especially the look on their faces, all pale and filled with dread. Then I saw Ben, grinning and nodding like he knew exactly what I was feeling. We both started to laugh and in no time the whole group was roaring uncontrollably. It took ten minutes of rolling on the ground, arms slicing wildly through the air, before anyone was able to stand. For weeks afterward the fear was echoed in all our laughter. Simple eye contact was all that was needed to set it off again.

The BB gun arrived on my thirteenth birthday—a gift from Uncle Leo. There was a brief round of concern and warning from my parents, and then I was pretty much allowed to do as I pleased with it. The introduction of a new weapon of terror was seen by the guys as a logical step forward. Bows and arrows were quickly and properly put into the past as we rallied around the gun. It took no great deal of discussion to decide what to do with it.

The game was simply called BB tag. The rules were minimal: one boy had the gun, the others tried to stay away from him. The shooter had to aim below the belt, a rule that caused as much dread as relief, and the "targets" had to remain in the open. The only benefit to being shot was that if you recovered, you were allowed to be the shooter. On a practical level we considered the possible consequences of the game, and when they seemed to be dangerous enough, we agreed to give it a try.

For a number of reasons, Tim became the most sought after target. First of all, at thirteen he was already nearing the six-foot range, and from our vantage point, legs appeared to be what he was mostly made of. A natural target. Tim's premature height also made him less agile than the rest of us: where we could turn on a dime, Tim required about a dollar-fifty. But the real reason we all liked to shoot him was the way he took the hit: sucking air through the enormous gaps in his clenched teeth, while holding his hurt leg as he bounced around the field like a one-legged giraffe. He took a great deal of pride in being the most popular victim; it gave him a unique status in the group. He took the pain, never complained, and wore his wounds like medals. At the end of the day he'd throw his stinging legs onto his bike and head home knowing he had endured the worst.

As BB tag worked its way into autumn we began to play the game less often. The last BB fired was a memorable one. It struck Ben. The best thing about someone getting shot was the dramatic presentation that announced exactly where the BB had struck. Except for Tim, insane chicken dancing done to the steady rhythm of teenage profanity was the expected standard; but when Ben was hit, he did neither. His body simply doubled-up as though someone had jabbed a bat into his stomach; then he slowly fell forward, making no attempt to break the fall. He hit the ground and just lay there curled up like a snail. He never made a sound. We gathered around him, voices lowered to whispers: "Hey, Ben? You all right?" After a long moment we heard a faint sound. We crouched lower, each of us holding our breath. We managed to hear just one word: "Balls."

"Hey, shit-for-brains."

The voice came from behind me. Ben had finally arrived.

I spun my bike around and pedalled out from under the bridge and into the morning sun. Ben was standing up by the road beside his bike, his body positioned squarely between myself and the sun. My first vision of him that morning was seeing his body surrounded by an incredible light. I squinted against the brightness. He seemed to glow with mysterious powers: a dark figure, defiant and bursting with energy. His legs were planted in the earth like the pillars of a tower, his head held high. As my eyes adjusted to the light I saw his long, straight hair hanging over his face, then the cocky slant of his mouth.

Something was up. Then I saw the rifle resting across his shoulders.

Ben's pose and the shock of seeing the rifle caught me cold, and he knew it. He stood there for a long moment, no doubt enjoying the look on my face. Then he took one long spaghetti-western stride in my direction, stopped, and while peering down at me, said in a cowboy monotone, "Just call me Ben Knutson, King Shit of Turd Island."

Ben had what my mom would call "a serious case of pottymouth." As soon as he thought adults were out of earshot, he would hardly ever say anything without swearing. Like most of the kids I knew, foul language slipped from his mouth with an ease I never could master. But unlike them, Ben's profanity was not limited to moments of anger or injury. For the rest of us, a great movie was, well, a great movie; but for Ben it was "a real shit-kicker," or if it was especially good, "a great cock-licker of a flick." If you didn't pay close attention to what he said, it was difficult to tell whether he was angry of just having a good time. When my parents asked why he was so quiet I told them he was shy, but I think the real reason he kept his mouth shut around adults was because he was never sure what might come out of it. Usually he'd just mumble something that even I couldn't understand. Everyone knew his dad was a real loudmouth. It was easy to tell when he was home because we could hear him hollering a block away. I saw him yell at Ben a couple of times, and all Ben did was mumble and start to leave. Then his dad would holler even louder: "What's that, boy? Something stuck in your throat? Sixteen years old and the dummy still can't talk!" He was a heavy equipment operator and worked all over the Prairies clearing ground for new highways. I had a pretty vivid picture of what he must have looked like sitting on a road grader, covered with sweat and dirt, farting, teeth bared as he tore into every hill, rock and tree in his path.

There were times when Ben would disappear for weeks, not answering the phone, absent from school. If I called at his house, his mother would come to the back door and say he was sick or out of town. She'd hold the door open a few inches with her bony fingers, only enough to let me see her face, like there was a dog or something behind her that she was afraid would get out. A regular sentry. Nothing was allowed in, and whatever was already inside, she was going to keep it there.

The way I saw it, Ben's life was already troubled in a way that I could never understand. Why he'd go so far as to take his dad's .22 was beyond me; it was sure lunacy. If his dad found out, there was no telling what might happen. I could imagine blood and broken bones, heads pushed through walls, police surrounding their house with blow horns in hand: "All right Knutson. We know you're in there. Let the kid go and nobody gets hurt." My mind was wild with fear.

"Man are you crazy? If your dad—"

"Ah," said Ben, the smug slant of his mouth gone. "The asshole left last night. Won't be back for a couple of weeks."

"Does your mom know you've got it?"

He looked at me for a second, the right side of his face flexed upward as if he were talking to his kid sister.

"Well of course she does." His voice deliberately light. "I've even got a note from her saying I got permission to ride around town with a loaded .22."

I knew it was a stupid question, but someone had to start thinking and it sure didn't look like Ben was going to. Did anyone see him coming here? How much noise would a .22 make? How would we get back through town later in the day when the streets are full of people? Questions came faster than my tongue could get them out. Then Ben jumped on his bike and started down the road.

"Time to hit the road, dork," he shouted, not bothering to look back as he sped across the bridge.

We headed south toward the flats by the river. I pedalled as hard as I could, but even though there wasn't much difference in size between us, despite my being nearly two years younger, when it came to strength, determination and just raw guts, Ben was pretty well untouchable. Whenever I got close enough to say something, he'd bear down on the pedals and leave me behind.

We turned off the gravel road a few miles out of town and followed the grassy trail that ended near a thicket of stunted poplars. By the time I arrived he'd already stashed his bike in the bushes and was digging through the pockets in his jacket. The rifle wasn't in sight. I was mad at him for taking off on me, and I wanted him to know it.

"Hey! What's the big hurry?"

"Shit!" he said, ignoring me, still searching his pockets. Then he began pulling them inside-out.

"Shit what?" I asked.

"I lost two of them."

"Two what?"

"Two goddamn bullets. I took ten, now there's only eight. Shit!"

"So what!" I said. "Eight gophers. Ten gophers. No big deal."

Ben stopped rummaging in his pockets, lifted the hair off his face and looked at me as though he had never really considered just how stupid I might be.

"Gophers?" he finally said. "You think I want to shoot fuckin' gophers? You're a regular fuckin' whiz."

I stared back, my insides shaking a hundred miles an hour. "So what do you think you're gonna shoot? Mountain lions?"

For a second I thought he was going to come after me, but then I saw the corner of his mouth start to rise. It wasn't exactly a smile, but I got the feeling he was enjoying the way I was standing up to him. I tried to keep up a brave front, even though we both knew I didn't have a chance against him.

"All I know," he said, "is I ain't wasting them on any stupid gophers." Then his face went dead. He turned and walked to an opening in the trees and stood looking out over the river. I stayed by my bike for a while, waiting for my insides to slow down, then cautiously made my way over to him.

Spring runoff had crested and the river looked like a huge gutter filled with mud. It was impossible to believe that in a month or so there would be sandbars and sun-warmed pools, and we'd all be out here running wild and leaping into the water. Ben squatted, picked up a stone and flipped it down the bank. When it disappeared into the sludge he looked across to the opposite bank.

"Guess I'm what you call a natural asshole." He was smiling and nodding in agreement with the description. "What the hell else can you expect from King Shit Knutson?"

"Well how about a few shots with that rifle?"

He stood, took a deep breath and looked straight at me. "But hey, we can't just start blasting away. Only got so many shells, and who knows what we might need 'em for—mountain lions, grizzlies, you never know."

He landed a firm punch on my shoulder.

"Yup, you never know," I said, returning the punch with a little more force than usual.

He grabbed his shoulder and hollered, "I've been hit! I've been hit!" He staggered back to my bike, let out a long, spit-filled gurgle which was meant as a death groan, then fell to the ground. As I stood over him, blowing the imaginary smoke off the fist that had done him in, I saw the rifle lying in the grass.

"You sure you won't get caught?" I asked, looking back at him as I knelt beside the gun. I could see his expression start to change, then he stopped himself.

"Relax," he said.

"Is it loaded?" My eyes were busy covering every inch.

"Hell no. Even I'm not that stupid." Then he got to his feet and began to push a runner through the loose dirt. "Musta fell out of my pocket coming out here. Damn."

I raised the rifle to my shoulder and pointed it out over the river. I had never held a real gun before. I was amazed at how natural it felt; the way the butt fit into my shoulder, how easy it was to hold. But most of all it seemed so simple to use, so comfortable, so innocent. Once my finger settled over the trigger, a gentle squeeze seemed like the easiest thing in the world. And the stock was beautiful. Not hollow plastic like my BB gun, but smooth, polished wood.

"Where do the bullets go?"

"Bullet," Ben answered, as he took the gun from my hands. "It only holds one at a time. This is where you load it." He slid the bolt back and showed me the hole. "You can use long and short shells, and you can get this other kind called mushrooms that have this little hole in the end, and when they hit something they go flat and make a hell of a hole. The old man didn't have none of 'em though."

We decided we didn't want to waste any ammo shooting cans, so we gathered our stuff and headed out along the upper trail. Ben took the lead with the .22, a shell in his hand, ready to be thrust into the chamber. I tried to maintain the appearance of an equally skilled and dangerous stalker, but every time my eyes fell on my BB gun I would lose heart.

We slipped through the scattered clumps of poplars, silent as moccasined Indians, cautiously scaled the small rolling hills, moving further out into the prairie, eventually losing sight of the river altogether. I fired a few pathetic shots into a flock of sparrows, but we didn't see anything that required the lethal power of the .22. With the sun shining high above us we stopped in a clearing to share what I had in my bag. I had just thrown an Eatmore to Ben when I noticed something in a nearby tree.

"Hey! What's that?"

"Where?"

I was already on my feet and after a few steps I knew what it was.

"A porcupine!" I shouted.

The porcupine appeared to be sleeping on a branch about ten feet up the tree. Ben came up beside me and we stepped closer.

"Don't go too close," he cautioned. "Those buggers can fire their quills twenty feet, easy."

It hadn't so much as blinked.

"Why doesn't it try to get away?" I wasn't so much asking a question as thinking out loud.

"Probably retarded or somethin'. Porcupines ain't exactly the smartest animal in the world."

"Maybe he's dead," I said, realizing too late just how dumb I sounded.

"Sure Matt," he said, leaping at the opportunity, "that's what all porcs do when they figure their time's up. Climb some damn tree so they can die up there and then fall off onto their stupid heads after. That way it don't hurt so much when they land. Right?"

He was looking at me, bug-eyed, head bobbing and mouth hanging open like a moron. I spun around and headed back to our stuff.

"I say we help finish the bastard off. Come on, get that cannon of yours loaded."

After spending the whole morning watching him carry the .22, I was itching to get my hands on it again. I picked up both rifles and turned and held them out.

"Choose your weapon."

Ben stopped suddenly, eyes darkening as he looked at one rifle, then the other, and then back at me again. He started to say something.

"Come on. Make up your mind!" What I needed was a decision, not a discussion.

He opened and closed both hands and raised his right arm. My eyes fixed on his hand, trying to will it toward the BB gun. Then he pulled the .22 from my hand. I had to keep everything moving.

"All right," I said quickly. "I've got a plan." I didn't want to think, didn't want any questions. "Let's try to pick it off from here."

Ben was standing as still as a post. I poked him on the shoulder. "Come on. Load up." He sluggishly slid a bullet into the rifle.

"We'll both fire at the same time. Okay? Knock the dopey retard right off that tree. You ready?"

He shrugged. It was all I needed.

I raised the BB gun to firing position and waited for Ben. When I saw the .22 settle on his shoulder I lowered my head and took aim.

"I'll count to three. Then we fire. Ready?" I didn't wait for a reply. "One, two, three!"

I squeezed the trigger. The BB gun let loose a spit of air, and a second later I heard the sharp snap of the .22. A clean, beautiful sound. A sulphery smell, but sweeter, like a freshly lit match or fireworks.

We both stared at the porcupine, neither of us knowing what to expect. Nothing had changed. The porcupine remained in the tree, motionless, as if we had never fired.

"Damn!" I exclaimed. "Must've missed him."

Ben's head slumped forward, his hair hanging over his face.

"Yeah. I guess so," was all he said.

"You sure you know how to shoot that thing?" I couldn't understand how he could have missed, not with a real gun.

"It's possible...I guess...that I missed."

"Can I have a turn?"

There was no response. He just stood looking at the dirt in front of him.

"Come on. Let me have a shot." I held the BB gun out to him. "Here, trade ya."

I waited for a second, then gently placed the BB gun against his leg. Very cautiously, as if trying not to wake him from a sleep, I lifted the .22 from his hands. He let me take it. It was mine now.

My hands shook as I fumbled open the bolt, and I laughed when the spent cartridge flew out of the rifle like a pilot ejecting from a jet.

"Bullets. I need bullets."

Ben pushed his hand into his pocket and when he opened his fist there were three bullets in it. I took them all.

"All right," I said, trying to inject some enthusiasm into him. "Now we'll see some action."

I closed the bolt over the bullet, cocked the rifle and raised it to my shoulder. I didn't care about Ben; I just wanted to blow that porcupine to pieces. My whole body began to shiver as I lowered my eye to the sights. Then the tiny brass ball at the end of the barrel fell across the still body of the porcupine. I took a deep breath and slowly squeezed the trigger. The rifle answered with another gratifying snap, and when I felt the firm jolt of the butt against my shoulder I knew I would never use the BB gun again.

I looked expectantly at the porcupine, convinced that it would either fall out of the tree or be thrashing on the branch. What I saw seemed beyond belief: in the tree, showing no sign of injury or movement, lay the porcupine.

"What the hell's going on?"

I pulled back the bolt to make sure the shell had fired. Everything was in order; the rifle had done its job. I must have done something wrong. I must have missed, just as Ben had.

I quickly covered half the distance to the tree, Ben muttering behind me. It would be impossible to miss from this close. I loaded the gun and focused right on the middle of its body and fired. There was an instant when I was certain the animal moved, but after taking a careful look I began to doubt what I had seen.

"This is bullshit!"

I grabbed a stocky piece of a branch off the ground and was about to hurl it into the tree when I noticed the red drips falling from the porcupine.

"Blood!" I hollered at Ben, sitting on the ground where I had left him. "Blood! Look. I did get it." When he started to stand I looked back at the tree. The blood kept dripping to the ground in a steady rhythm. *Splat. Splat.* A bright pool of red had already spread across the decaying leaves.

Ben came up beside me, his face still blank as he looked at the body in the tree. Then he turned to me, his eyes moving slowly from my face to the branch in my hand.

"Well, Matt," he said, staring at the piece of wood, "I think it's dead now. You can beat it with that club if you want, but it ain't going to get any deader."

I found another branch, a longer one, and moved under the tree. I was certain the porcupine was dead, but I kept remembering a dog that I had seen get hit by a car the summer before. The rear legs had been crushed, and I guess the car had driven right over its stomach because the intestines looked like they had been shot right out of its butt. But the dog wasn't dead. It kept trying to get to the other side of the street, dragging its guts and legs through the dirt. It was unbelievable. So when I raised the branch under the porcupine a part of me still needed to be convinced it was dead. I gave it a sharp jab and stepped back—there was no sign of life. I could tell Ben was getting ready with another wisecrack, so I quickly went back and pushed hard. Down it came, landing on its side, face turned under its body and buried in the dirt and leaves. I was convinced.

We both knelt beside the body, voices falling to a hush.

"Wow, he's a lot bigger than I thought," I said. "Does anyone eat porcupine?"

"Nah. Indians used to, I think. I don't know."

He lifted a leg and turned it carefully in his hand.

I wasn't interested in feet—I wanted to find the bullet holes. I picked up a stick and lowered it into the quills. The blood was pretty thick and I had to scrape it out of the way to see the skin. And there it was, a hole, just in front of the shoulder. It wasn't half the size I expected.

"There," I said. "See?"

Ben put the leg down and looked. Then I saw another hole, a little lower and behind the shoulder.

"And another one, back here." I worked the end of the stick into the second hole and began stretching it open. "Do you think the bullets are still in there?"

Ben shrugged.

"Let's check the other side." I stood, placed my foot under the body, and rolled it over. There was plenty of blood, but I couldn't find any holes. I was sure the bullets were still inside the body. I got up and ran back to my knapsack.

When I returned Ben was holding the porcupine's head between his hands like he was talking to it.

"So, what's Porky got to say for himself?" I asked.

"Look at his face," he said.

All I wanted was to get in there and find the bullets. But I squatted beside him, hoping that if I played along he'd stop being so weird.

"What d'ya see?" he asked.

"I don't know. Hair. Whiskers."

He was acting like a teacher, as though he only asked the question because he knew there was no way I'd have the right answer. I didn't want to play along.

"You see something I don't?" I asked, trying to get it over with as fast as possible.

"Well...it's sort of like he's, I don't know, kind of simple." He spoke carefully, the whole time staring hard at the porcupine's face. He said something about the quills, and how they weren't there to hurt anyone. But I couldn't follow him. It was taking him forever to get the words out, and all I could think about was finding those bullets. It was pretty obvious I was wasting my time—he wasn't going to start acting normal. Then he looked at me and that was it: he just dropped the head, stood up and walked toward the bush.

"Hey, where you going?"

"I gotta go to the can," he said. And then he disappeared.

I sat for a bit, staring at the porcupine and trying to see what the big mystery was. Then I remembered the bullets. I dug my knife out of the knapsack and rolled the porcupine onto its back.

The previous summer my dad had taken me fishing up north and it was there that I learned to clean and fillet fish. Once I knew the basics I began to focus on speed. I wanted to be the fastest fish filleter in Saskatchewan. Every evening I'd meet the boats on the dock and offer to clean the day's catch as a way of sharpening my skills. The whole time I never once thought of a fish as anything but slime and scales, and they certainly didn't have faces. I didn't expect there to be any difference between a fish and any other animal.

I placed the point of the knife on the belly, just above its butt, and pressed. The hide was tougher than I expected, but once the blade had cut through I was able to work the knife under the skin, pulling the blade slowly upward, careful to avoid the quills. I could feel the body heat rise through the opening and over my hands. When the cut seemed long enough I wedged a stick into the opening and began to search for the bullets.

Small pools of blood had gathered in the hollows between the organs. The intestines were easy to identify, but there was no way I could tell the difference between a heart or a liver. A smooth, bulging shape in the lower abdomen caught my attention. It was bigger than anything else and covered with muscle. I shifted the intestines to the side and began cutting into it. There was some kind of membrane under the muscle, a thin layer that looked a bit like a clear plastic bag. When I touched it with the knife it just fell open and a cloudy liquid began to drain out. I stretched open the remaining muscle and peeled back the membrane. Horror swept over me when I realized what I was looking at. Curled up inside the cavity was an almost perfectly formed miniature porcupine. *Oh God*, I thought. *It's a baby. I killed a baby!* I heard Ben coming out of the bushes behind me. I wanted to hide the porcupine or run away, but I couldn't move. Then his footsteps stopped.

"Man you're sick. I can't believe this."

He moved closer.

"You kill the damn thing, then you have to carve it up too?"

He was standing beside me now.

"I thought you—"

And then he stopped. He must not have seen the baby porcupine until then.

I turned to him, wanting to apologize for everything. His eyes were frozen on the porcupine, his face a sort of greenish-white colour. Then his body pitched forward, like when he had been shot in the balls, and he puked, much of it falling on his pants and shoes as he staggered backward. When I stood he gave me a threatening stare and yelled, "No!" Then he grabbed the .22 off the ground and ran toward the river.

It was all my fault. I had kept pushing and pushing. I wanted to go after him and make him pound my face in. I wanted someone, anyone, to see what I had done and then knock me senseless.

But I stayed in the clearing, mostly just walking around wondering how I got to be so stupid. Before I left I dragged the porcupine into the bushes and covered it with leaves.

When I got back to my bike I went over to where Ben had stood looking out over the river. I didn't even look at the BB gun and I didn't stop to see how far out it went. I just grabbed the barrel with both hands, swung it around once then let go.

I didn't see much of Ben for a while. He rarely came to school and I was too ashamed to phone him. Whenever I did see him he made a point of staying clear of me, and I guess I acted pretty much the same toward him. But in the middle of the night, about two weeks after the porcupine incident, I was awakened by tapping on my bedroom window. I stumbled out of bed and peeked through the curtain. There he was, standing in the shadow of the neighbour's house. I quietly slid open the window.

"Hey, what's going on?" I whispered.

"Matt, I need some money. You got any?" His voice was serious.

"Yeah, I got a little. How come? What's up?"

He picked up a garbage can, set it below my window and climbed onto the lid. When his face was level with the window I saw the bruise on his left cheek. His hair was matted in spiky clumps and there was so much blood on his ear I had to look twice to make sure it was still there.

"Geez, are you all right?"

"Yeah. Sure."

"What the hell happened."

"My old man came home tonight. Started makin' trouble for Mom, drinkin' and pushin' her around again." He pressed his lips together and looked behind me into the darkness of my room. "I couldn't stand it no more, just lying there. So I went upstairs and told him to leave her alone. He just looked at me and laughed. Then he threw her across the room, starin' at me the whole time, just daring me to do somethin'. Mom could hardly talk but she kept telling me to go back to bed. Then he said, 'Yeah boy, better go beddie-byes,' and started after her again. I don't know. I called him a bunch of names, and the next thing I know, Mom's screamin' and I'm goin' head-first down the stairs."

"God. You should call the police."

"I found this pipe in the basement," he said, staring straight ahead, not even hearing me. "I don't think he even knew I was behind him. It was real easy now that I think about it."

"Jesus, did you kill him!"

"Nah, but I'm pretty sure I busted his leg real good. I didn't stick around and now I'm leavin' for good."

"What do you mean? Where you going?"

"Anywhere. But I haven't got any money. How much ya got?"

I raced through the room emptying every pocket and jar I could find.

"Looks like about twelve bucks," I said, handing it to him.

He cupped the money in his hands and began to climb off the garbage can. "That's great."

"Hey, where you going to go?"

"I don't know. Maybe work on a ranch or join the rodeo, be a rodeo clown or somethin' flashy. Who knows?"

It sounded like a real plan to me.

He started for the back alley, then stopped.

"Hey Matt?"

"Yeah?"

"Thanks."

"No problem."

"Not for the money."

"What for then?"

"Ah, ya know. For...stuff."

I watched him slip through the back gate, then he turned and disappeared down the alley. A few seconds later his voice came rushing through the darkness: "Whooo..."

THE VAST AND GREATLY HUGE

Two months had passed since Keith almost died. He'd been stung on the lip by a bee while working in the garden. Anaphylatic shock, that's what they told Margo later at the hospital. He'd just been able to make it to the house before collapsing. Luckily his brother and Margo were there. They laughed when he careened through the kitchen door like some gothic monster, one hand wrapped around his neck, the other pointing frantically to his gaping mouth. Keith's reputation as a prankster was legendary. The Olympics were on at the time and they'd all gotten into the habit of scoring everything—the weather, meals, movies. Keith received a 7.9 from his brother and a 6.5 from Margo. They weren't impressed.

Keith's sense of humour was especially directed at scaring the hell out of the people he loved, and Margo was his prime target. It wasn't simply the challenge that drove him on, and there was more to it than just an inability to resist temptation. No, for Keith, the mind was like an antenna, constantly receiving signals from a place he smilingly referred to as "the vast and greatly huge, I know not where." He had an image in his mind of an undulating wave of energy, the very pulse of existence, flipping and flashing through space like a giant, spiralling cord. He liked to think of it as the channel through which all thought came into being—the DNA of intelligence. And the most appropriate response to these unbidden thoughts was to act on them as quickly as possible. He had a few pat routines, such as climbing onto the roof after one of his late-night hauls to Vancouver, and then making just enough noise to rouse Margo as he crawled through their bedroom window. But his greatest satisfaction came from assailing her with a multitude of spontaneous antics, all of which revolved around death. So when he stumbled into the kitchen, wheezing and grasping at the air in front of him, they hardly bothered to take notice. When he fell across the table Margo just looked at her brother-in-law, shook her head sadly and made a comment about insanity running in his family. What eventually got her to her feet was the sound Keith's head made when it landed on the hardwood floor.

Within minutes they were speeding to the hospital. The doctor said Keith would have died if they didn't live so close—said it was a one-in-a-million reaction. Keith was in the emergency room at ten in the morning—unconscious, a nurse squeezing air into his lungs using an ambu bag—and home for supper by six. "Quite a day," he'd chirp whenever someone brought it up. Margo still tells everyone about it—grocery clerks, waitresses, vacuum cleaner salesmen, anyone who'll listen. And she laughs the whole time she's talking; quietly at first, but by the time she gets to the end her eyes are flooding her face and her laughter has transformed into a high-pitched cackle that you can hear a block away.

The sun is shining through the window in the kitchen and Keith is wiping the lunch dishes and singing along to Neil Young's "Down by the River." Whenever the chorus comes around he turns to his son, Ned, bouncing in the Jolly Jumper, and does his famous impersonation of Joe Cocker: his body hunched forward as he blindly staggers across the kitchen; then suddenly he's reeling high above the boy, head and arms shaking, palms up and fingers twisting into the air, and his voice erupts in a series of rasping and precarious notes. Then he swoops down, rubs the dish cloth on the boy's face and they both howl with laughter.

Keith is halfway to Ned, waving the cloth in the air, just working up to the *I shot my baby* line, when Margo bursts through the back door.

"Keith! Keith!"

He spins around and she's on top of him before he can even think.

"I just got stung by a bee," she cries, her voice climbing out of control. "Right here on my neck! What were your symptoms?"

Margo's eyes are wild with fear and she's biting her bottom lip and hopping like she has to pee really bad.

"It's okay," he says, trying to sound reassuring. "Hardly anyone has a reaction like mine." *One-in-a-million*, he thinks to himself.

"What were your symptoms!" she demands.

"All right. All right," he answers. "Let me think." But the only thing Keith can think about is Margo, how scared she looks, and how funny she looks when she's so scared.

"Oh yeah. Right," he says. "Hands. I had itchy hands."

Right away she starts to scratch her palms and it's all he can do to keep from smiling. Her head is nodding in agreement.

"Yes! Yes!" she exclaims. "My hands, they're itchy!"

She's working back and forth now, first one hand and then the other, the skin instantly scored with white scratches. She's still bouncing on one leg.

"What else?" Her whole body jerks with each word.

He's fighting to appear serious. "And my feet and head, they were itchy too."

The words are barely out of his mouth and she's rubbing her scalp with one hand and untying her shoes with the other, still hopping.

"Oh, God! No!"

She's fallen to the floor now, the shoes are off, her hair is a hive of knots, Ned is screaming in his Jolly Jumper and Neil Young starts in with "Cinnamon Girl." Keith can feel a rhythm in the chaos, a marvellous pattern of sound and movement—a field of energy gathering around them, leading them somewhere. He yells into the din, "And they were hot. God, they were hot!"

She's rubbing her legs and flapping the bottom of her sweater.

"Quick, take me to the hospital," her voice childlike, sobbing. "I'm gonna die!"

She starts to get to her feet but before she can stand he quickly adds, "And there were hives, hives all over my arms and chest."

Margo drops to the floor, yanks out the collar of her sweater and stares down her chest. Keith steps to the side and manages a laugh that is eaten up by Ned's screaming and a raunchy guitar solo.

"Ahh!" comes the cry from under the sweater. "Hives! Oh God, no. I've got hives!"

She rips off her top, stands and runs to him, her breasts bouncing freely in the sun-warmed air.

"Look!" she shrieks, a finger pointing above her left nipple.

He leans in for a closer look, eyes widening for additional affect. He can almost see her heart pounding, like a fist inside her chest. Her body is running with sweat; her acrid scent is everywhere. He breathes deeply, as if to steal this one moment, this one memory, for only himself. He touches her breast, rubs a fingertip over the tiny red spots. There are three of them, very small, not half the size of pimples.

"You see them, don't you?"

"Hmm," he says, trying to approximate a doctorly tone, then nodding as if in deep thought. "There's only one other thing."

"What? What is it?"

He places an arm around her waist and pulls her to him. Her skin is cool and clammy; her eyes twitching. Everything has been so perfect, so hugely perfect. He can see how desperate she is to know—how terrified she is to find out. She shivers against his palm and he can feel the energy converging into a vortex of impulses, the currents arcing around them like thin tongues of light. And he can't stop himself.

"Sex," he says. "An incredible desire for sex." Then he falls to his knees in an explosion laughter.

But then there are hands circling his neck, cutting into his flesh, choking off his voice. He opens his eyes and all he sees is her mouth screaming into his face, "Take me to the fucking hospital right fucking now!"

Keith is sitting in a chair in the emergency waiting room. It's unbelievably quiet, like a morgue he thinks, or perhaps the hospital has been allowed a moment's rest from the world. Every once in a while someone covered in white or pastel green slips quickly past him. He listens closely, following the squeak of the rubber soles as they gradually fade away down the hall. Ned is sleeping in his arms and Margo is being moved to a room on the second floor. The doctors aren't sure if it was the sting; she had some of the symptoms, but not others. They're not worried about her; she's going to be all right. But they wanted to keep her overnight, just to be sure.

When they arrived, Margo had charged into the hospital, past the other waiting patients, past the receptionist, yelling, "Anaphylatic shock!" Keith stood in the middle of the hall with Ned whimpering in his arms as the staff swarmed around her. It was a magnificient spectacle: Margo, though paralysed with fear, sweeping her arms in the air like some mad duchess as she bombarded them with a detailed description of what had happened, when it happened and all the symptoms that followed. By the time they had moved her into a curtained area she was telling them about the hives on her chest and Keith's reaction two months earlier. The last he saw of her was just before the curtain closed. She was sitting on a gurney and had just pulled her sweater off. It was only a brief glimpse, but it was all he needed—the red blotches were easily the size of silver dollars. Then she disappeared. Keith couldn't make out what was going on, but he could hear her repeating "Oh God! Oh God!" from the other side of the curtain. Then someone ushered him into the waiting room.

He has been sitting for a long time, holding Ned, listening, waiting to find out what he should do next. And even though Margo is nowhere nearby, the sound of her voice still echoes around him. *Oh God!* And her voice, when taken just by itself, stripped of bee stings and hospital curtains, seems more a summons to passion than anything said out of fear. It seems even more curious when he thinks of having pulled her to him, half naked and trembling in the kitchen, and what he'd said about wanting to have sex being the last sure sign. Stranger still that the length of time from then until she disappeared behind the curtain would have been the same had they been making love. And now, sitting under the antiseptic glare of hospital lights, surrounded by tile and metal and silence, afraid to move lest he wake his son, he can't stop thinking of her breasts coming toward him in the kitchen, the sour smell of her body, her skin, damp and cool in his hands. *Oh God!* It's as if he's fourteen again, sitting in church or the back seat of his parents' car, unable to stop the urgent rush of blood, the swelling. He's not exactly sure what he should do. It's so quiet and bright, and everything—the chairs, walls, the elevator doors—all of it suddenly so heavy, so large, so stable. But he knows he won't be able to keep a straight face much longer.

HABITS AND LOVE

The grand finale, which took over four decades to perfect, usually began around one or two o'clock in the morning when Wally would creep into the unlit living room, his silver-streaked hair shining in the glow from the street light in the front yard as he dropped side one of *The Coldstream Guards Marching Around the World* on the stereo and cranked the volume until the speakers rattled. When the marching drums exploded into the room he would face the hallway while marching on the spot, his right arm locked in rigid salute, and wait for Bea to come hollering down the hall. A lifetime of discipline lay beneath the simple gesture of dropping the needle onto the record, eliciting the desired effect it had on Bea.

With some people, you need to go over a lot of territory before you find out how wrong your assumptions are about them.

In the early years they would gather at the Air Force Association Bar at the airport. They were a curious mix of cohorts: one-time pilots, navigators and ground-personnel, most of them from flying schools in Manitoba that were already showing signs of neglect. But it would be a mistake to believe the war had injected every one of them with patriotic virtue. For Wally, the war had been an opportunity to learn to fly, something he'd only been able to dream about as a child of immigrant parents who had no inclination of wanting to own a car or alter the humble old-world habits of their native home. As far as he knew, his father had never gone higher than climbing the ladder into the attic, where he cured his homemade sausage next to the chimney. During his training, Wally's heart wasn't beating with patriotic yearning as he pretended to swoop down on a mile-long caravan of German supply trucks, or at night, when he guided an Anson bomber over the red flares near the border of Saskatchewan. What lay beneath him was irrelevant. His fascination had everything to do with the openness that spread out around him: the unobstructed space, the freedom to fall and climb in any direction. And for three short years he had lived the spacious dream of his youth.

These were the days they were making the transition into civilian life, and the Air Force bar was the middle ground between where they had been and where they were going. They haunted the bar wearing the uniform of businessmen—heavy grey or brown suits, conservative-coloured ties, leather shoes shining and ready for inspection—junior clerks, salesmen, and servicemen, the rank and file who, in Wally's circle, would soon leap into management positions in the burgeoning Credit Union system and its pseudo-twin, Federated Co-op. A few of the men had kept their pilot licenses after the war, and on weekends they would rent a Cessna or Piper Cub for a few hours to keep their logbooks up to date. Wally had befriended a few of these men, and when Bea was off in another corner of the bar he'd often wander over for a chat, or send a round of drinks to their table, always with the hope they'd invite him on their next flight.

Most of the young brides were no strangers to military bars and some, like Bea, had joined the service and worked as military clerks or beside the men in the war factories in Regina and Winnipeg. For Bea, patriotism was an appealing refuge from being the oldest of nine children in a destitute family: all those bodies crammed into a ramshackle apartment overlooking the harbour in Port Arthur; diapers strung across every room, like the flags on the ships outside the window; a father who worked for the railroad, a ghost really, for he never seemed to stay home for more than a day at a time. She knew the Germans were supposed to be evil. She saw the pictures in the papers, the headlines, the news reels at the cinema. But that war was far away, in another world, a different galaxy; and she was here, now, eighteen years old and sharing a bedroom no bigger than a closet with two sisters, constantly cleaning and cooking, breathing the same stale, used air that was silently but surely killing her mother. She knew the Germans were supposed to be evil, but then again, they might have been a lot like us, maybe even too much like us. It was silly and frightening to think such things, but she did, though never out loud. Besides, she had her own war to contend with. A week after turning eighteen, she pinned a note to the bathroom door: *Gone to fight Hitler. Bea.*

She left the service with a firm command of the King's English and Wally pinned like a medal to her arm. She was two months pregnant and three months shy of her twentieth birthday.

Back then smoking was an innocent indulgence for anyone old enough to shave or wear stockings. Twenty years later Bea would still dismiss all medical evidence to the contrary. "A pack a day and three kids," she would later say whenever anyone brought up the dangers of smoking, "and they all got a brain and an asshole." And beer was like Kool-Aid for adults, though Wally, who had travelled into the neighbouring states and provinces, called Saskatchewan beer skunk piss. Every time another round of Big Chief or Red Ribbon landed on the table he would fill the top third of his glass with tomato juice to kill the taste. But drinking beer was mostly a Monday-to-Friday ritual for Wally, and going to the bar was little more than a warm up for the serious partying that would take place at home.

After a few hours of darts and shuffleboard, they would make their way over to the house. Wally, normally a shy man who will spend most of his working life driving from one end of Saskatchewan to the other, sleeping in motels and checking security alarms in every hick town from Val Marie to La Ronge, always invited everyone at the table to come along.

He waits for her to go down into the family room or to the bathroom, then he appears in the kitchen with a broom in one hand and a serving platter from the china cabinet in the other. The regulars have mixed reactions. The men drop their heads or reach for a drink in an attempt to suppress their laughter, not wanting to give the innocent victim too much of an idea what lies in store, while the wives shake their heads or make half-hearted attempts to call Bea back into the room: "Bea! Get in here. Wally's at it again." But no one tries very hard to stop him.

Then he singles out someone in the group, a newcomer and a man, like the others before him, who knows nothing about what is about to take place.

"You ever see a plate get stuck on a ceiling?"

The women respond instantly, "Don't listen to him," slapping the backs and shoulders of their husbands. "And you, you stop encouraging him." The men snort into their glasses.

The newcomer doesn't want to be the one to dampen the mischievous twinkle in his host's eyes. He likes these people, their constant noise, the way they banter so easily back and forth, the men pairing off against the women, both sides imagining there is a trench between them. It doesn't matter if he is married or single, he knows the war must continue at all costs.

"Bea!"

Wally doesn't wait for an answer. He's already pulling a chair into the centre of the room, pretending to fumble the platter while eyeing the ceiling.

The women gasp on cue: "Jesus, Wally! Bea is gonna kill you!"

He ignores them as he studies the ceiling, searching for the precise spot to place the platter. But Bea will be back soon. He can't take too much time. Without looking down, he hands the broom to the newcomer: "Hold that for a second." The man stands and takes the broom, thinking he's no more than a spectator. Wally lifts a foot onto the chair, then heaves his body upward. Every movement is accompanied with a grimace, a grunt, some exaggerated gesture that never fails to get a rise out of the women. For an instant he teeters too far to the left, threatening to fall onto the middle of the table. Arms grab at bottles and glasses. Someone leaps forward to save him. But he's already corrected himself, and when they realize it's just another one of his pranks, the room erupts.

He towers above them, the china platter securely in his left hand, pretending to be disheartened by their lack of confidence.

"I need another drink," he says, but then he hears the toilet flush. The platter is quickly raised to the ceiling, right above the newcomer, with the bottom facing the floor. Again, without looking down, he asks for the broom, places the tip of the handle under the platter to hold it flat against the ceiling, and moves both hands down the shaft.

The smiling newcomer looks around the table. They're all shaking their heads. No one looks at him. Light spills into the hallway as the bathroom door opens. Then Wally's foot taps against the newcomer's shoulder. He looks up.

"Hold this while I get down," says Wally. He stands and holds the broom. "Use two hands. And keep the pressure on it."

Wally steps down, slides the chair over to the table and sits down just as Bea walks into the kitchen. His timing is impeccable. The men applaud him. He toasts himself. The newcomer, now abandoned in the centre of the room, holding the china against the ceiling with a broomstick, finally catches on. And once again, Bea hits the roof.

"My china! Goddamn you, Wally."

"What did I do?" He's the picture of innocence, a boy trapped in a thirty-two-year-old body. Even the women can't stop from laughing.

"If that falls, I'll break your bloody head open."

He looks questioningly around the table: "What did I do?"

The man holding the broom shuffles and Bea shrieks, "Don't move!"

Wally leans back in his chair, astonished. "I'm just sitting here having a drink—"

"I'll give you a drink, mister."

"—minding my own business—"

"That's the big platter, isn't it? You put my big platter up there, you stupid ass!"

Wally looks up at the ceiling, eyes widening in surprise. "Holy shit," he says. "How'd that get up there?"

Someone breaks into a coughing fit from laughing so hard. The newcomer is obviously hoping this will end soon. His arms are starting to quiver. He'd like to sit down.

Wally gets up and circles the chair in the middle of the room while studying the platter. He stops in front of the man holding the broom, his face bent into complete bewilderment as his eyes move down the wooden shaft until they meet the newcomer's. "What the hell are you doing?" he asks.

The man smiles uncertainly.

"That's Bea's china platter, you know. She loves her china and her crystal and her silverware. Don't you, Bea?"

"Just get it down in one piece, Einstein." She lights a cigarette and stares at him through the smoke.

Wally shakes his head in disbelief, muttering, "I give and I give and I give," as he drags another chair from the table.

"I'll give you something, mister," says Bea.

"I got plenty already, thanks." He climbs onto the chair. "But you could pour me another drink."

One of the husbands reaches for a bottle, then stops when he catches Bea glaring at him.

The platter is safely retrieved from the ceiling, though not before Wally, once again, feigns falling off the chair. Bea takes it to the dining room, places it on the shelf of the hutch and does a quick inventory before heading back to the kitchen. The newcomer thankfully returns to the table, where he is met with a fresh drink and a round of applause from the men.

"Last time it was the gravy boat," someone tells him.

"And that guy from Yorkton. What was his name?" But they're all laughing again, except Bea, who is still perfecting the brutal scowl she will always be remembered for.

There's nothing worse than a dull war. Slogans like "Some chicken; some neck" are mandatory. Uniforms and weapons need to be upgraded. The audience back home has to be kept in a state somewhere between potential disaster and heroic optimism. A good war is never an accident.

Just after midnight Wally is once again swaying in front of Bea's prized hutch. It has taken him several years to work through the entire china collection—the various serving bowls and platters, the gravy boat, the butter dish, dinner and dessert plates, creamer and sugar pot, saucers and cups—and not so much as a chip of damage. It's time to move on. But the crystal goblets are too risky, and an evening of wearing the punch bowl on his head and pretending to be Captain Video from *The Honeymooners* pretty well exhausted its use, never mind the trouble he had getting a drink to his mouth. All that is left are Bea's bowling trophies from the ladies' Tuesday morning league — three of them lined up on the top shelf, each with a minuscule, plastic woman sprayed in gold, her perfectly shaped little body arrested in full swing, mounted on a cube of imitation marble. And there's the silverware, of course, neatly filed away in the drawers. But what could he do with that? Pin Bea to the kitchen wall and throw the knives at her?

A voice breaks over the din in the kitchen: "This pirate comes into a bar..." Wally wanders through the dining room and stands alone in the middle of the living room, already smiling at the end of the joke Mel has only begun telling.

"...wooden leg, a hook for a hand, a patch over one eye..."

Just standing in the living room was enough to get Bea going. After the basement had been finished the living room was zoned off limits to everyone except Bea, who ruled the area with uncompromising authority. This was the one corner of her world that proved she had successfully cast off the screaming babies, the toddlers with fevers and snotty noses, the plywood over the broken windows. Twice a week she would dust the maple coffee- and end tables, fluff the throw pillows always strategically placed to resemble diamonds in the corners of the new colonial couch, and then conclude with a thorough vacuuming of the white carpet no one was ever allowed to set foot on.

"...the guy beside him is going crazy..."

Once a month she shook the curtains, sprayed and wiped the mirror over the couch and the picture window, through which she could look out at the neat rows of new houses, wiped the sills, the family pictures on the ledge by the door and the three-foot, translucent orange vase Wally had given her on their fifteenth anniversary. Bea's immaculate room was a shrine, a still-life of order with an imaginary silk-tasseled rope hanging across the entrance; though for Wally and the kids an electric fence would be a more fitting image. If *Good Housekeeping* ordered a surprise inspection, Bea would be ready.

"...'Yahaar, matey,' he says. 'I was swinging o'er the Spaniards' ship when a rope caught me by the leg...'"

All he has to do is turn on a light and Bea will charge out of the kitchen, promising him a slow and painful death if he so much as puts his glass on the coffee table or sits on the furniture. But simply being caught in enemy territory, even if it is the sacred heart of Bea's existence, requires no imagination. Any moron could turn on a light.

"...the best swordsman in all Europe, he was..."

Then it comes to him, and less than a minute later he is standing at the entrance to the hallway, waiting for Mel to get to the punchline.

"...'Hell no. That was the day after I got the hook put on me arm!'"

When everyone bursts into laughter Wally steps out of the living room, clamps shut his left eye and takes the first step of what will eventually be known as his Pirate-from-Hell routine.

Maintaining his balance and walking a straight line with one leg stuck in the three-foot-high glass vase would never be an easy feat. There was easily enough room to stand on the bottom of the vase, but his leg was too thick to fit all the way in. It was like having one leg six inches longer than the other. And the weight was incredible. From the very beginning he always had to use both hands to swing the beast in a half-circle for each step. But the effort more than paid off when the glass leg hit the linoleum with a resounding thump.

They're all laughing at Mel's joke when he reels into the kitchen. No one has noticed the glass leg yet, but Wally already knows he's back in business.

The weekly gathering spot has moved across town to the Legion, where the Pirate-from-Hell routine has boosted Wally to the rank of Captain in the minds of all the men. Now whenever he steps through the door he can't go more than ten steps before someone lets out a loud "Yahaar!" and for the following fifteen seconds the bar is turned into a galleon of chanting pirates. As soon as they start, Bea's arm swings into action, repeatedly whacking Wally on the back of the head while threatening to do the same to every man she passes: "That's what you all need. A good smacking!" The men are quick to respond: "Come over here and smack me, I'm a *baaad* boy!" and "When do I get my turn?" and "What are you doing tomorrow night?" Fellow Legionnaires keep coming to their table, handing Wally eye patches, bandanas; someone even gave him a life-sized plastic parrot and offered to hot-glue it to his shoulder. One night a complete stranger introduced himself to Bea by trying to shake hands with the bent end of a coat hanger sticking out of the arm of his jacket. Bea shot out of her chair as if she had grabbed a snake, everyone roaring their consent, some for the quickly retreating stranger, others for Bea, who stood cursing and panting with both hands pressed over her heart. She spent the rest of the evening developing a profile of who the man was, where he came from, and how he knew about Wally's routine. By the time they were ready to go back to the house Bea had the stranger pegged as a brown-nosing bank clerk from Butt Hole, Saskatchewan, and was convinced Wally had set the whole thing up. All the while Wally sat at the end of the table making question marks with his shoulders, saying, "What did I do?"

Now each time they gather at the house, Wally notes the expectant looks, the raised eyebrows, the men nudging each other whenever he stands. Everyone is watching and waiting, hoping this will be the night he'll once again come stomping down the hall with the glass leg.

But Wally doesn't always give them what they expect. Some nights he talks shop for hours, telling stories about the flimsy security systems in small-town Credit Unions. How the managers think a deadbolt on a wooden door and a five-hundred pound safe bolted to the floor are all the protection they need. He says a couple of farm boys would have no trouble cleaning out two or three of them in one night. He says the security company he works for is going to make a fortune in Saskatchewan. Other evenings he's happy just to sit at the table, quietly sipping rum while Bea blitzes him with her rapid-fire comments. He knows he doesn't have to pillage the china hutch or walk up and down the stairs with his leg stuffed in the vase to get her going. All it takes are a couple of drinks and she's quite capable of carrying the evening alone. Her list of complaints is endless: the Indians in the duplex across the alley; how the house needs repainting; that the men's choice of clothing stinks. She calls them cheap bastards and eggs the women to join her. Wally gets it in the ear for taking a coil of garlic sausage out of the refrigerator: "Put that stinky crap back. You're not sleeping in my bed tonight, mister." Then he gets it again for not cutting it up and putting it on the table. Ten minutes later he's a wisenheimer for pointing out she has just bitten into her second piece. Never a dull moment. Bea, his sidekick, his straightman, the grande dame of one-liners.

But Wally is careful to pace his entrances. He knows every performance, no matter how spectacular, has its limits. And that is why he has waited for the right moment to add a new wrinkle to the famous routine.

Tonight the men in the kitchen raise their glasses and sound the rally cry of "Yahaar! Yahaar!" when they hear the familiar sound in the hall.

Bea spins off her chair, instantly, faithfully, and begins to circle the kitchen, waiting for her target to appear.

Wally hammers the vase onto the linoleum and returns the call: "Yahaar!" He has learned to rotate the vase with each step in order to gain speed and how to stagger the force of each impact by using the edge to produce a serviceable threat, then shifting his weight and bringing the full radius of the bottom of the vase to the floor when a more terrifying effect is needed, such as now.

Thump!

The kitchen is a carnival of movement and noise: the men genuflecting and cheering their returned king; the women cowering in mock terror; and Bea, dependable as ever, yelling, "You idiot. You goddamn nincompoop," and waving a fist in Wally's face.

Wally puts on a dazed look, his head following the back-and-forth motion of Bea's fist.

"*Sleeeep. Sleeeep*," he says, eyes fluttering, body sagging forward.

"I'll put you to sleep, all right."

It looked like another of her usual punches, hard enough to get a person's attention without causing any real damage. Every man in the room had received at least one of her corrective blows in the past, and they all knew a quick shot to the head was as close as Bea ever came to a declaration of affection. A punch in the shoulder meant you were under consideration; a knock on the head and you were in her good books. It wasn't a hard or particularly well aimed jab, and if her fist had rotated a few degrees either way nothing would have happened. But the crown of her diamond ring landed perfectly on Wally's jawbone, and within seconds a trail of blood began to roll down the front of his neck.

Wally touches his chin, then stares with amused surprise at the red liquid on his fingers. "I've been hit!" he exclaims.

"I warned you," says Bea, now back in her chair, arms and legs pulled tight to her body.

Mel stands and tips Wally's head back to get a good look. "She got you good this time. Stitches maybe. Hard to say."

"I need a nurse," says Wally, then he swings the glass leg into action and heads for the stairs.

"Use the downstairs bathroom," shouts Bea, staring at the far wall as he passes. "I don't want you dripping blood in the good bathroom."

"Yeah, yeah."

"And take that bloody thing off your leg."

"Yeah, yeah."

Everyone except Bea watches him lurch and bang his way to the split stairway, where he pauses and looks toward the basement, then upstairs, and again back to the basement. They all know what he's thinking and none of them are surprised when he begins to hop up the stairs, dragging the the glass leg behind him as though it were a dead body.

Bea has her back to him, but she can tell what he's doing by the way Mel is biting his lip to keep from smiling.

"I said the downstairs bathroom!"

"I need a nurse."

"You need a brain surgeon."

"Nurse! Nurse!"

Everyone drinks and smokes faster than usual while Wally is in the bathroom. Someone notices the blood on Bea's ring and knuckles, and after washing her hands in the kitchen sink, she starts emptying ashtrays, wiping the counters, washing glasses. Every few minutes Wally stops slamming the drawers and cabinets long enough to yell for a nurse, or a medic, or a drink, occasionally for all three. Eventually Mel's wife, Anna, picks up his glass and heads to the bathroom, excusing herself by saying someone has to do something to shut him up.

"Make sure he cleans up his own mess," yells Bea, furiously attacking a blob of dried mustard. "I'm not running a hotel here."

"Medic!"

Anna disappears up the stairs. They hear her break into hysterics the moment she enters the bathroom. The noise continues to roll into the kitchen in broken waves, and between the swells they can hear Wally's wheezy laugh, his ruptured attempts at whispering which are swept away by another flood from Anna. Something falls. A bar of soap? A jar of hand cream?

"Sounds like they're really going at it," says Mel.

"That Wally," replies one of the husbands. "A regular Casanova."

"A regular jackass, is what you mean," says Bea, her voice seeming to test some new-found frequency, then fading to a near whisper. "Or a jackrabbit... yeah, that's it, jackrabbits. That's what they are." She pumps her pelvis once, then plunges her hands back into the sink.

They all look at her for a second, waiting for a punchline that would never be delivered.

Five minutes later Wally is standing at attention at the bottom of the stairs, the orange vase slung against his shoulder as if it were a rifle, an enormous wad of toilet paper held under his chin by two bands of white tape that have been wrapped around his entire head. The door to the bathroom remains open and everyone can hear Anna peeing and gasping for breath.

He returns his boisterous reception with a look of inflated seriousness.

"I believe," he announces, carefully picking holes in the wall of laughter. "I believe I've co-ag-u-lat-ed."

Bea takes one look over her shoulder, shakes her head and turns back to the dishes. She wipes the steam off the window over the sink and Wally's reflected image appears in the centre of the glass.

"Your brain is coagulated," she says to the window.

"Returning for duty, Sir," says Wally, eyes front, still standing at attention. "It's nothing—a scratch, a mere flesh wound. Nothing a drink can't fix."

"I'd like to get you fixed, all right. Permanently fixed."

"Left face!" he calls out, briskly turning toward the hall leading to the living room. "Forward march!"

Bea watches his reflection merge into the dark hall, yelling after him, "Stay out of my living room."

"Yeah-yeah, Sir!"

The window is a far cry from a mirror. She can't see exactly what he's doing, but she can tell where he is by the white tape circling his head. He goes straight for the living room, but just as Bea is about to take action the white stripes reappear in the hall. He's busy taking something from the hall closet.

When he finally comes into the light, the vase is gone and he's wearing a suit jacket, buttoned at the middle, but the left arm is empty and hanging loose. His right hand is buried in the pocket. With his head wrapped in toilet paper and tape he looks like an war amputee just released from the hospital. Everyone knows something is up.

"Where's my drink?" he asks. He pulls his hand out of the pocket and places a miniature of the orange vase on the table. It's only eight inches high, but identical in shape and colour. They're all amazed at the similarity. Even Bea leaves the sink to see what everyone is looking at. She picks it up and makes a curt inspection, her face showing no sign of softening.

"Hey, be careful with that," says Wally, reaching across the table for a bottle and winking at the wives. "It's *ex-treeeme-ly* fragile."

Bea gives him one of her *up yours* looks and puts the vase back on the table. If he had brought it out any other time she might have given him a chance. But not now. Not in front of everybody. Not with the toilet paper and tape, and now the jacket and who knows what else.

"What's the deal?" she asks.

"No deal," he says, unscrewing the cap on the bottle.

"*Humph!*"

"That's it? That's all you have to say?" His face tumbles into a dramatic pout, which is quickly replaced by a wince as the tape tightens under his chin.

"I got plenty to say," replies Bea, turning away from the table. "I'm saving it up." She opens the drain in the sink, reaches for a towel.

Wally, still grimacing, puts the bottle down and fingers the toilet paper under his chin.

"Uh-oh!" says Mel. "Sounds like she's not finished with you."

"She never finishes," says Wally, this time winking at the men and in a way that suggests there are other issues at stake. Their heads bob in silent assent to the common suffering of husbands, and Wally pours two fingers of rye into the tiny vase and offers to top up any empty glasses.

"Where are my cigarettes?" asks Bea, wedging herself back into her chair at the women's end of the table.

Wally raises the vase to the ceiling light, taking on the guise of a connoisseur of fine wines. Despite all the bandages, the absence of one arm gives his figure a strange dignity. He slowly swirls the rye inside the orange glass and inhales the aroma from the narrow opening. As always, he ignores the guffaws of his audience. His flourishes and tableaus are confined to the stage of serious art, where composure and consistency are mandatory. The vase is once again raised to the light for a final scrutiny before he tips the contents into his mouth.

The whole time Bea fiddles with a cigarette, pours a drink, organizes all the glasses and bottles and ashtrays within arm's reach. By the time she's run out of things to do everyone is yakking and laughing, and Wally has come over to the women's side to show them the vase, talking in a way she knows is pure baloney. He's setting them up again, that much she knows. The men know it too, for aside from the occasional quick whisper, they've stopped talking and are following Wally's every move.

He's standing between Beth and Anna, his hips nudging their shoulders, holding the vase waist-high and going on about the fine detail, how the glass-blowers must have to make dozens of them just to get one that comes out perfect. He's managed to get them to turn away from the table so he can point out the smoothness of the sculpted lines, the consistency of colour. As their heads bend closer to the vase something pink darts out of the fly of his pants. The women scream and rock the table, then they're right back for another look. The table threatens to buckle as the men lean forward. Everyone jostles for a better view, except Bea, who has remained in her chair, smoking and muttering "idiot" and "jackass" to no one. The top of the vase is buried inside Wally's fly, and through the orange glass they can just make out the fleshy shape lying inside the neck. Wally starts to pull the vase away and all hell breaks loose. Beth and Anna jump to their feet, shrieking and stumbling over each other as they attempt to escape. A glass tumbles to the floor and rolls into the middle of the kitchen. The men are hooting and pounding the table. Wally takes one step backwards and tugs at the vase again. The ruckus increases instantly. He twittles the vase again, this time turning it as if it were the volume knob on a stereo and the room is wild with hammering fists, rattling bottles, Anna threatening to pee on the floor, coughing and choking and howling. One of the men shouts out that he's going to have a heart attack. Then Wally jerks the vase away, revealing the index finger of his left hand dangling from his fly. He wiggles it a few times, then points it to the ceiling and starts walking toward Anna, who is doubled over by the stairs. Panic strikes when she sees him coming, and she bolts for the upstairs bathroom, her legs glued together at the knees. Wally looks around the kitchen, his masked expression of confusion twitching like a dam about to rupture. He catches Bea's eye.

"What did I do?"

Bea throws an indifferent glance at the finger still aimed at the ceiling. "At least you got the size right," she says, talking to no one in particular, then turning back to her drink.

The women roar. The men wince. And Wally collapses into a slump. They all stare at his crotch, the finger drooping steadily downward, coiling in on itself, then slowly wiggling back into his pants.

"You've hurt its feeling," he says, stretching the fly open and peering inside. "I think you killed it."

"One down, a million to go," she says.

"A drink," he proclaims, extending the vase at arm's-length to the men. "A drink to the walking wounded."

"Yahaar!" responds Mel, reaching for the bottle of rye. And then they all join in: "Yahaar! Yahaar!"

After years of service work, Wally has shifted into the sales end of the business: safety deposit boxes, free-standing signs announcing current interest rates in red plastic letters, wall racks for investment brochures, real and imitation security cameras, coin and bill counting machines. Drive-up banking windows have been a hot item for the last couple of years, not just in Regina and Saskatoon, but even in places as small as Melfort, Estevan and Humboldt. Within a few years he'll be buying most of the windows back at a fraction of the price, storing them in the garage until he finds new buyers in Alberta or Manitoba. His travel schedule is down to three days a week, with the rest of his time spent on the phone, ordering parts, typing invoices and price quotes, sending out brochures, filing reports to the security company's head office in Toronto.

On Thursdays at 1:00 Bea has him drive her to the hairdresser. He wanders through the mall, checks out the day-old bread, the loss-leaders, then brings her back home. At 3:30 she calls up the stairs: "It's time. It's time." He emerges from the bedroom-turned-office and walks out to the car to take her downtown.

She's working one day a week, 4:00 til 9:00, in the shoe department at The Bay. It's her first job since the armament factory in Regina during the war. All the way there she's busy talking, lighting cigarettes, checking the time, arranging. The car fills with smoke, perfume, hairspray.

Wally sits. Drives. Rolls down the window. He always has a letter or a package to put in the downtown drive-up mailbox, or a business he can call on, just to keep in touch.

He stops in traffic. She jumps out. The separation is free of "See you tonight," or "Have a good day," or "Bye."

At 9:05 he returns to pick her up. They go to the Legion. Have a drink. She complains of her aching legs, her back, the smelly feet and greasy hair she had to put up with, the teenagers loafing around the escalator; how rude people are, how they're impossible to please and that she shouldn't even try. Her voice circles his silence like attic air.

He wonders what to do with his elbows, drinks his beer and tries not to remember that he'll probably never fly another plane. He considers ordering another drink. He keeps an eye on the door. Watching for someone he might know. Anyone.

In the fall of 1968 Wally attempts to add a new move to the pirate routine by goose-stepping across the kitchen while the men chant *ziegheil* and give him the straight-arm salute from the sidelines. Halfway to the fridge he misjudges a step and the top of the vase explodes around his lower thigh. He spends all of Sunday in the basement trying to glue the pieces into place, and early the next morning, just before he leaves town, the vase is restored to its designated spot in the living room. When Bea sees it later in the morning, she places it in the darkest corner of the room and fills it with bulrushes and Chinese grass to hide the damage. He will move it only one other time, but Bea will not be there.

On their twenty-fifth wedding anniversary the kids give them a specially engraved silver platter and organize a huge party in their honour. The Leisure Land Hall will fill with friends and relatives who have come from as far away as Ontario to celebrate the occasion. A deejay plays fox trots, polkas, Led Zeppelin and The Beatles until 2 a.m. In the middle of the festivities, Wally and Bea are called on to stand together at the front table. The hall is silent. All eyes are on them. Like children thrown into the spotlight, they speak briefly and haltingly about their life: how they met when they were both in the service and married in Winnipeg during the middle of the war; then how they moved to Saskatchewan in 1949. Bea lights a cigarette while Wally introduces the friends from the early days who have come all the way to Saskatoon to be with them tonight. They thank their kids and everyone there for a wonderful night. A long silence follows as they stand two feet apart and look nervously out at the crowd. Then one of their kids begins to tap the rim of a glass with a spoon, and soon everyone is joining in. Even from the back of the hall it's easy to see their faces flush as they turn and dutifully kiss, eyes wide open, arms motionless at their sides. It's over in half a second. A few of the younger people try to work them up for another round, but Wally cries out for another drink and Bea is already moving away from the table.

The console stereo arrived on Christmas Eve, 1969. It was the final detail to complete the colonial theme Bea had begun years earlier with the hutch (which was closely followed by the solid maple dining room table and chairs) and had spread into the living room with the addition of the couch and chair and ottoman, and the matching coffee- and end tables. Bea had Wally rearrange the room so the stereo was as close as possible to the hall. Having a fine stereo was one thing, but she wasn't going to allow anyone to traipse through the whole bloody room just to turn it on. The real satisfaction for her came from simply seeing her room finally complete, and now that the last piece of the picture was dropped into place, the whole family was expected to do no more than stand at the entrance and gaze in silent admiration. But Wally had other ideas, and within the year he had a small collection of records and the stereo became the dominant force in his Saturday night struggles.

Glenn Miller owns the stereo for the first year and Wally has trained the men to stand on his command and pretend they are the boys in the brass section. He usually calls on them when Bea launches into one of her rants about something he has done or could have done or should have done. When she starts to get wound up he focuses on the music, waiting for the exact moment when he visualizes Miller pointing to the back row of the band, making sure they are ready. Then he snaps his head up and he and the other two or three men jolt from their chairs, swing their imaginary trombones, trumpets and saxophones into position and go to it. Wally's chosen instrument is the trombone, and he makes a point of aiming it straight at Bea's forehead, using the full length of his arm to slide the brass tube violently back and forth. On those rare evenings when he thinks Bea is not carrying her weight, he keeps ordering the men to their feet, three, four times in a row if needed, and pumps his arm at her until he sees the familiar glow in her eyes.

It's been a good night for Wally. Mel and Anna are back from two weeks in Hawaii. Then Leonard, from the main office of the Credit Union, and his wife, Beth, arrived with two managers in training, young fellows in their early-to-mid twenties with polished, windburned faces. Wally can tell that, unlike Leonard, who with little more than a high regard for military order had worked his way into management by pragmatic perseverance, these boys have formulas and theories running through their heads. He's sure that, if asked, they could recite the Gross National Profit for the last ten years. But right now they're just two young fellas about to break into the world and eager for as much fun as possible before being sent into the toulees. Within minutes of arriving the one with the boyish face is blessed by Bea's knuckles.

"Watch out for her," Mel tells the trainee as he rubs his shoulder. "Keep your head up, eyes open and stay out of the corners."

Wally has the new recruits happily settled on the men's side of the table with their drinks topped up. Glenn Miller is swinging away in the living room, and before the first side of the record is through, Wally's got them jumping to their feet with the regulars the second he commands the brass section into action.

Bea leans across the table and tells the young men to ignore Wally. "He's just a worn out old fart," she says.

Wally tunes in to the music, hears a meandering clarinet leaping across a soft, shuffling rhythm. The timing is all wrong—he knows he can't call on the band to squelch her.

"If I could do it all over again...," she says, her eyes blinking in and out of focus, rolling lazily from face to face, then finishing the sentence by flicking her hand at Wally and blowing air from the side of her mouth. Then she shrinks back into her seat, her head bobbing in self-absorbed conversation.

Wally asks the trainees if they have an idea what town they'll end up in. They appear relieved with the question, but they don't have a very definite answer. Canora. Wilkie. Esterhazy. The names drop onto the exact spot on the map of Saskatchewan Wally has in his head. They've also heard rumours about Nipawin, and both of them make sure Leonard isn't watching before cringing at the possibility. He tells them to let him know where they go so he can send them tickets to the Riders' games, then adds under his breath, "Even if it is Nipawin," knowing full well it's a four-and-a-half hour drive to Regina. They nod in unison, earnestly, slowly, calculating, as though conscious for the first time of the perks soon to be conferred upon their rank.

"Here's one," says Mel, slapping the table to get their attention.

"Why do tornadoes always strike trailer courts?" He taps the finger-tips of both hands together three times and adds, "They're attracted by all the bowling trophies."

Wally sees Bea's face darken with contempt, her eyes flashing over his head to the trophies on the top shelf of the hutch in the next room. For her, nothing seemed innocent or unintentional anymore, and at times, he was hard pressed to separate her staged and garish responses from her reckless and often unintelligible assaults. But this time he knows what is going on in her head: how she has taken Mel's joke as an affront to her past; that people who bowl are basically telling the world they have no brains, no future, no class; that trailers are the modern breeding ground of the ignorant, and no different than the slum apartments of her childhood in Port Arthur. And because Mel knows her history, she'll convince herself that his joke has a larger purpose: that behind the china, the crystal, the silverware, the colonial furniture, the remodelled living room, despite everything she has gathered to separate herself from her past, she will never be able to disguise her shabby roots. She will always be the oldest daughter of an itinerant railroad worker and a mother who was constantly pregnant and barely able to read.

"It's Harry time," Wally announces, hoping to create either a diversion or get out of the room before Bea leaps for Mel's throat. He is on his feet and heading for the stereo, paying no attention to the muttering rising from the opposite side of the table.

Belafonte at Carnegie Hall, 1959, a two-record album of the most treasured music Wally will ever hear. He places both records on the stereo, careful to arrange them in the proper order, and watches the bottom disk fall onto the turntable, the stylus swinging out. A moment of anticipation. And then the roll of kettle drums, trumpets and applause as Harry walks onto the stage, the orchestra slipping through a twenty second-medley, then giving way to the acoustic guitars, an upright bass and bongos. There's no melody now, but the rhythm is compulsive, alluring, infectious. Wally turns up the volume. Adjusts the bass. His head twitching, toes tapping. Then Harry starts in: *Wake up, wake up*—drawing out the last word on a single note, a lure spinning through the air on a thread of silk—*darlin' Cora*. Wally is not in the living room; he is not listening to a record. He is somewhere else: he is in the audience, he is flying solo above the clouds, he is the man in the moon.

Mel appears beside Wally just as Harry starts into his jazzed up version of "Cotton Fields Back Home."

"Christ," says Wally, still staring at the stereo, "that bastard can sing."

"I thought maybe you died."

"What's that?"

"You've been gone ten minutes. Left me alone with Bea. She's on the war path."

But Harry's magic is still working, and Wally is snapping his fingers, doing a little soft-shoe on the carpet, singing along: *I was over in Arkansas, when the Sheriff asked me, What did you come here for?* Mel is with him instantly, both of them clapping and singing. They shuffle into the hall, two white guys from Saskatoon, on the downhill slide from middle age, shuckin' and jivin' as best they can: *In them there, oh, cotton fields back home.* Mel garbling the beginning of most of the lines and trying to make up for it by belting out the familiar endings. When they enter the kitchen, Wally pulls Anna from her chair and starts dancing her around the room. It's an unprecedented move. Wally dancing! Mel takes up the challenge and goes after Bea, who rarely hums let alone dances, but she brushes him away, refuses eye contact, preferring instead to mumble and nurture her resentment over his joke. Mel grabs Beth instead, and they join Wally and Anna, the four of them clapping and falling into each other in the small space in the centre of the kitchen. The recruits, their arms looped over each other's shoulders, are swaying back and forth and wailing to the music.

Before the song ends, Wally is back in his seat, panting and holding his hip and insisting that one of the young men get up and finish the dance with Anna.

"Leave them alone," says Bea from across the table.

"I think I pinched something," says Wally, wincing, rubbing his hip, then reaching for a drink. "I need pain killer."

"We were having a discussion," she says, her voice sour, veering suddenly to reproach as she narrows her eyes on the recruits, "Weren't we?"

They look searchingly at each other, as if having missed out on something obvious.

They're saved by Beth and Anna appearing with a broom and holding it at waist-height and hooting as Mel attempts the limbo. He fails miserably.

"Ignoramus," says Bea, to no one.

Then Beth has a turn, removing her shoes and easily succeeding at the initial height. The men cheer. Harry starts in on "Day O." The broom is lowered a few inches and again she is triumphant. At the next level Anna enters the ring. A heated debate takes place as Mel, acting as official judge, objects to a new competitor joining the contest so late in the process. But the young men, while butchering a variety of German, French, Russian and Swedish accents, launch into a rigorous explanation of the international rules governing track and field, citing the high jump as the relevant event in relation to the limbo and inventing a list of historic precedents from previous Olympic Games held in Congo, Iceland and Hawaii. Leonard, proclaiming himself "The Chairman of the Whole Goddamn Olympic Thing," hammers his fist on the table, strips Mel of his judgeship, and orders him to shut up and hold the broomstick or he'll have him removed from the area. Bea offers her support by raising her glass to Leonard. From the living room, Harry injects a similar logic into the fray, and Wally sings along in a loud voice: *If the woman the other, and the man the other, and the ton-ton pull but the lemon grass.* Mel complains about kangaroo courts, dishonourable discharge, due process, but Leonard's decision is final.

The contest continues, and after two rounds the broom is nearing knee-height and both women are still in the running. Anna has a classical approach, silent, fluid, her face almost void of expression. She shifts one foot ahead, then the other, her progress measured in minuscule advances. Beth has a hard-edged, labouring style, lots of grunting, her face straining, lips pinched between teeth as she hops and jerks forward on both feet. But they're both amazingly agile.

A look of satisfied lassitude washes over Beth when Anna fails on her next try. Beth proposes a tie, but the men will have none of it: "A winner must be crowned" and "The gold must be claimed" and "How low can you go?" Leonard's managerial fist seals the verdict.

And there is Bea, half watching from her chair, her face set with dramatic, forced unconcern—a new look, one that will always demand too much self-discipline, too much of a reversal to ever be successful. For Bea, silence and pretending disinterest could never be weapons. After marching in one direction for so long, after all the theatrics, the ridiculing, the provoking, it's impossible to think you can simply turn around and head out in a new direction. Wally has seen the look more often lately, as though she is searching for some new advantage. It's often one of the last things he sees at night, even when he's on the road. He could be lying in a motel two hundred miles away and there she is, a hologram floating above the bed: the grim, thin-lipped mouth, the eyes struggling to fight back the wary and insinuating glances, the poorly concealed readiness to take offence. After living under her brutal scowl for years, this new look, this facade of unconcern, will gain little more than a small corner of the battleground they share. It will never merge into Wally's expectations of her, of himself, of them. She will test it from time to time, but it fits her like a borrowed dress, a secondhand pair of shoes. Its minor usefulness is limited to the sphere of privacy, those few days a week when they are both home alone, or late at night after the company is gone.

Beth begins her descent, but only after making it clear that it's a one-shot attempt, "Do or die," as she says, and her celebrated career as Queen of the Limbo will be over regardless of the outcome. Leonard is standing now, abandoning his neutral status as chairman and cheering and staring in disbelief as Beth, his wife, this woman he has lived with for over half his life, contorts and heaves and grunts her way under the broom stick.

Bea glances quickly, indifferently, at Beth, whose body is cantilevered at the knees and almost parallel to the floor. "You show 'em, honey," says Bea in a voice that falls purposely short of encouragement. Her deliberate unconcern is now meant to suggest she has always been privy to Beth's miraculous and hidden strengths. She is treating Beth's victory as a foregone conclusion, so there is no need to celebrate the obvious. She will view it no differently than any other fact. Her refusal to show surprise is intended to convey her superior understanding of the intricate fabric of life, her abilty to observe with ease what others fail to understand at close scrutiny. But Wally has seen enough of this look to know it's the ludicrous clarity that only a fool would claim. For how could Bea, who bowls on Tuesdays, watches soap operas all week long, who rarely reads a newspaper—how could a woman who sells shoes four hours a week at The Bay see herself as having a vision of anything? It would be fine if she had taken on the role for comic purposes, but over the years her extravagant rage over his pranks has gradually fallen away. If she wants to provoke laughter now, it is always at someone else's expense, not hers. And the more she refuses to play her role, the more determined Wally is to up the ante.

Beth falters as her breasts, two islands rising from a sea of white cotton, nudge against the broom. She's not a large woman, but her wired bra is definitely doing the job it was intended to do. Mel extends an eager hand and offers to flatten them. She barks back at him to hold the broom tighter, and for the next few seconds the world is confined to two breasts being squashed beneath a wooden shaft; then an eruption of cheers as the islands reappear in their former state on the other side. Leonard clears this throat ceremoniously and glances at the two young men, their faces flushing under his futile attempt to regain a professional poise. And then she's through and being helped to her feet.

"Miraculous!"

"Unbelievable!"

"Whoop-dee-doo!"

"A victory parade!" proclaims Wally, thrusting a drink at Beth. He wedges her between himself and Mel and they begin marching in a tight circle, hands cupped to lips, imaginary horns squawking. Anna and Leonard fall in at the rear while the recruits beat out a foot-stomping rhythm on the table. He leads them down the hall, calling out, "Right turn," as they veer into the living room, all of them wailing and tromping, Harry pitched into chaos, the needle bouncing and scraping across the record as they turn the corner into the dining room, leading them twice around the colonial table and chairs, then a final pass in front of the hutch, Wally hollering, "Eyes left!" and all of them following him by sharply saluting the china and crystal and bowling trophies before completing the circle and reappearing in the kitchen.

And there is Bea, a bundle of spite on her chair, legs crossed, arms wrapped over her chest, tenacious in her defiance, her eyes reduced to mere slits and targeting Wally's every move. For the next hour she will cling to her dark resolve. The men stay clear of her. Wally passes a cautionary look at Mel as he stops behind her on his way to flip the records on the stereo. They leave it to the women to bring her back into the fold, offering her cigarettes and drinks, questioning her about the kids. "How is Bobby doing at university?

What is he taking?" and "Is Annette still dating that bozo from Ontario?" Bea will be marginally civil, dutiful in her answers, but she will not play her part, neither for them nor for Wally. She will not allow any of them to defeat the malice she has fought so hard to earn; twisting the bitterness she has nursed for so long into the only victory she can claim as her own.

All rivalries are to be neutralized, recessed, ignored for a time. It's a standoff, a momentary ceasefire. An onerous lull closes around them. They're in limbo. The sound of loose chatter. Mel describing the beaches in Hawaii. Leonard going over some banking details with the recruits. Wally sipping his rum and Coke, closing his eyes and tipping his head back, imagining a world filled with clouds, listening to Harry, occasionally singing to himself: *I wonder why nobody don't like me? Or is it a fact that I'm ugly?* All of them waiting, testing the balance of the evening. It's just after midnight, still early for a Saturday night, but late enough that they could leave without disgrace, claiming early-morning duties—driveways and sidewalks in need of shovelling, visiting parents, Sunday dinners, taking kids to hockey practice—the ordinary, unimaginative lies we use to fool even ourselves. Beth and Anna continue to coddle Bea, hoping to bring her back to life so they can either leave without feeling guilty or stay and start over. But Bea is in no hurry. She is the unacknowledged centre of attention, gathering whatever pity she can to herself like a sulking child. She's changing all the rules and Wally isn't about to accommodate her. Not after all these years. Not after spending all week alone in his office or driving around the province in sub-zero temperatures, eyes straining against all that whiteness, stopping every hour or two, waiting half an hour to have a fifteen minute conversation with the local Credit Union manager. Then back to the car, the snow washing across the highway...thirty...forty...fifty thousand miles a year.

The recruits are starting to fidget, and it sounds like Mel is threatening to recount yet another holiday in Hawaii. For Wally, hearing about the obligatory winter getaway to Hawaii is like having a hamburger at McDonald's: you can keep going back, but it's always the same. He could fake interest in just about any topic if he were working or at the Legion or the Air Force Bar; he knows when to offer an encouraging nod, a knowing smile, how to angle his eyebrows to express surprise. Diplomacy is the artifice of all worthy salesmen; but he's home now, in his castle. This is the one night they are supposed to play by different rules, and if Bea has her way much longer, he knows the house will be empty in no time. Even Belafonte seems to be pressing the evening to a close by starting in on "Matilda," the last song on the record.

He tries the chorus on the young men, waving his arms like a conductor to cue them, nodding strategically: *Matilda she take me money and run Venezuela.* It's supposed to have a crescendo effect, get their blood pumping. They give it a try, but they're too polite, too civilized, too obediant, too sober. What he needs is a full frontal assault.

"The audience," he tells them, directing a thumb at the wall separating the kitchen and living room behind him, then standing and moving from the table, "listen to the audience. Going nuts. Got them eating out of his hand." And he's gone, half-running down the hall. A moment later Harry and the audience are coming through the floorboards—rattling the walls, shaking their intestines—and Wally is back.

The women are cringing, cocoons in their chairs, hands over ears, complaining in short blasts of noise that can only be understood by the pain on their faces.

Mel is pointing to the living room, hollering about the speakers on the stereo.

"Fifty watts!" yells Wally, pretending to grab his penis. "Fifty watts of Harry! The full nine yards!" And Mel, laughing, shaking his head.

The chorus is coming around again. The song is almost finished; he knows he has only a couple of minutes to get things back on track.

His arms rise into the air, ordering the men to attention. He should have done it half an hour ago, should have done it as soon as she started changing everything.

And they follow him, out of loyalty or duty or suffering, their voices barely discernible in the din. But it's a good enough start for Wally. And with Harry blaring away, there is no way Anna and Beth can keep pampering Bea. *The money was to buy me house and land, then she got a serious plan*—hovering above them, his arms like wings slicing through the air, lifting, leading—*Matilda she take me money and run Venezuela.* He can hear them this time. They're coming together: Leonard's head bobbing to the rhythm; the recruits loosening up under Mel's encouragement.

The women have given up trying to talk and Bea is sitting upright, precise, motionless, elbows on the table and staring at Wally, her face flushed with rage. It's a good sign for Wally. He's brought her back from the bowels of self-pity. She'll go on full attack now. The balance will be restored. He returns her stare, bulging out his eyes for extra effect, inspiring her to action.

Her lips move. Not just a word or two, but a complete sentence, the first one in almost an hour. It's impossible to hear her, but the consonants are so obvious, the syllables so clearly formed and punctuated. Hearing is irrelevant.

He turns back to the boys, rousing them toward the final chorus, his arms thrashing. On cue, all of them howl like coyotes, then stand and bow to each other while the audience applauds and whistles its approval.

The women are gone. Bea. Beth. Anna. All of them. Their chairs empty. Nothing left but the damp rings on the table where their glasses were. Anna just disappearing into the family room in the basement. The stereo falling silent. Their ears ringing.

They look at each other, not sure if they've succeeded beyond their wildest expectations or blown it completely.

"Uh-oh," offers Leonard.

"What's the problem, Lennie?" asks Mel, smirking and leaning halfway across the table. "Afraid you won't be getting any tonight?"

Wally joins in, "Or tomorrow. Or the next day. Or the next..."

Leonard shakes his head, smiling too easily.

"Not that I blame you," says Mel. "That limbo stuff. Who would've thought. Gave me a bit of a woody, too." Then turning to the young men, their shining faces quickly reddening. "How about you boys?"

They pull themselves to attention. Squirming. Clearing throats. Their minds racing, realizing there is no safe answer. The older men allow them five seconds of devastating silence before breaking into fits of laughter. Leonard hooting, "Not bad for a couple of old broads, eh?" and holding his glass high to toast his good fortune. To this they agree eagerly, without hestitation, nodding their consent and reaching for their glasses.

Then Mel gasps and slams his palm on the table. "Maybe Wally will lend you boys that broom for the night." And they're all killing themselves, Leonard's drink spraying from his mouth, Mel hacking, Wally wheezing, the two recruits finally free to join in.

Wally pours everyone another round, their colluded laughter dividing, trickling away.

"What they go down there for?" asks Wally, faking innocence as he tips his head toward the basement.

"Haven't the slightest," says Mel. "Maybe they don't like Belafonte."

"Everybody likes Harry."

"Think so?"

"Know so," says Wally. "Have to be deaf not to."

"What's that?"

"I said you'd have to be—" then checking himself and punching Mel's shoulder.

Leonard offers to go downstairs, "Just to investigate." But Wally and Mel see right through him.

"Stop letting the little head do all the thinking," says Mel.

"Five bucks says I can have all three of them up here in two minutes," says Wally. "Without going downstairs or saying a word."

"You got a secret weapon?"

"Always," says Wally.

"How you gonna do it?"

"Secret."

Mel turns to the young men, his voice dropping, pretending to take them into his confidence, "Resourceful guy, this Wally. A good friend to have when they drop the big one. Either of you boys have a watch." They both nod and pull up their sleeves. "Now, if you've got five bucks that you've been itching to throw away..."

"And you're not going to say a word?" asks Leonard, calculating, looking around the kitchen for some clue. "Or go downstairs?"

"Nein!"

"The man's foolproof," says Mel, pulling a bill from his wallet and slapping it on the table. "We're not playing to win, boys, we're paying to watch. Trust me. Captain Wally is our man."

As they dig for their wallets, Mel and Leonard fill the young men in on Wally's glorious history: the china on the ceiling, the Pirate-from-Hell and the One-Armed-Peckerman routines, the exploding vase, the night he ate half of the mother-in-law's tongue that sat in front of the picture window in the living room, Bea's tumultuous tirades, her right hook. All the while Wally is hustling to the hall closet, the back door, his prankish, wheezing laugh ever present. He returns, lays two mops and the limbo broom on the table.

They're all thinking: *China. He's going to get all of us to do the china trick.*

Mel reaches out, one hand stroking the black bristles of the broom, his eyes rolling back in his head, moaning louder and louder as his other hand slips up the shaft. Leonard calls him a sick bastard and pulls the broom from his reach.

Wally stops at the foot of the stairs, motionless, his face bent in concentration.

"Shh," whispers Mel, his hands freezing in mid-air. "The Master is thinking."

And then he's on the move again, back down the hall, rumaging in the closet. He comes back carrying two short sections of steel tubing from the vacuum cleaner, keeping one for himself and adding the other to the mops and broom on the table and says, "One each, gentlemen. Choose your weapon."

Leonard quickly claims the broom, flaunting his victory at Mel.

Mel, with a look of inflated concern, turns to Wally, his voice assuming the brisk resonance of military life, "Sir!"

"Yes," answers Wally, instantly following Mel's lead.

"We have a mission."

"We do."

"There are risks?"

"Women are involved."

"There are dangers?"

"Women are involved."

"May I speak candidly, Sir?"

"You may."

"Sir. Leonard should not be allowed to have the broom."

"Why?"

"Because he's horny, Sir, and he thinks it's his wife."

The young men start laughing. Wally glares at them, collecting his whole body into an over-the-top version of a deranged drill sergeant. "Is that true, Leonard?" he asks, still bearing down on the recruits, who, taking on their assigned role, shrink under his stare and fall silent.

"He was touching it, Sir. He—"

Mel butts in, suggesting Leonard take the vacuum tube and go relieve himself in the upstairs bathroom.

"A woody," says Wally, forcing a moment of quiet reverence by gazing as if in fond remembrance at the far corner of the kitchen ceiling. "A woody is a terrible thing to waste."

"Here, here," offers Mel, raising his glass to Leonard. "To wasted woodies."

"To those who never died in action."

Wally hurries toward the hall, calling over his shoulder, "Gentlemen, prepare for duty."

They stand and wait, listening to the low voices of the women in the basement. Wally playing with the stereo. The slap of a record falling on the turntable. Then Wally, rounding the corner, fiendishly buoyant, air spewing between his teeth. There is a loud, grating hiss as the needle makes contact. Wally grimaces, raises his shoulders, presses his head down into his body, preparing to duck, and issues a warning: "Bombs away!" The stereo explodes with marching drums, a thousand of them, storming through the walls, the men squinting, recoiling.

Wally turns back and faces the invisible onslaught, the tangible noise, the vacuum tube hoisted, rifle-like, and hollers, "Forward march!"

They move out, following their leader single file, paying no attention to the rhythm, not marching in-step and swinging their arms; instead, they move forward by the sheer will of each man to think past the mind-numbing crush of drums.

"Right turn!" And they cross into alien territory. Mel is right behind Wally, followed by Leonard, who hesitates at the entrance to the living room; but the innocent recruits stagger into him, laughing, oblivious, pushing him forward. Mel and Leonard suddenly understand Wally's battle plan. He is going after everything all at once: the full-meal deal; an all-out attack; the whole mishmookama.

"Two minutes!" yells Wally, steering them into the dining room, knees pumping. "Two minutes!" But the horns have arrived, piercing through the percussion, the house is a battlefield of noise. It's impossible to hear Wally; impossible to recognize the tune.

He turns into the kitchen, hoping to see Bea; but no one is there. He executes an about-face and waits for all four men to stumble in behind him. The Coldstream Guards are well into it now. There's no excuse. He waves his arms to get their attention. Ten seconds later they're marching on the spot, basically together, stepping in unison if not to the rhythm. They head out for another round, the recruits doing their best to call out the steps.

When they complete the circle Beth and Anna are at the top of the stairs. But there's no sign of Bea. He continues past them, inviting them to join in, ignoring the threatening looks that stop Leonard in his tracks, that tell him to corral the two recruits.

Wally is back in the living room, making a beeline for the ottoman, unaware that his troop has been reduced to Mel, who already realizes his participation in Wally's schemes will land him on the couch for the night, woody be hanged; Mel, who is already arranging the story of Wally's latest escapade, watching Wally prepare to mount the ottoman, seeing the outragous foot slam into the cushion; Mel surprising even himself, slowing, faltering, stepping around the ottoman, turning toward the dining room and catching out of the corner of his eye someone standing in the dark hall, the red glow of a cigarette, and knowing instantly, despite his drunkeness and without having really seen, that he had saved himself, maybe. And Wally, never once looking back, alone and lurching toward the kitchen. Mel follows, muttering into the incomprehensible racket, "Bombs away."

And it is about to begin—the grand finale, the ceremonial march that Wally will use now, and again, later, whenever Bea refuses to play her part.

Leonard, without seeking permission from Wally, turns down the volume on the stereo. The house collapses into an oppressive silence.

Bea is standing in the centre of the kitchen, seething, her new brutal scowl perfected, but she's still refusing to attack. The recruits are the first to leave, receiving nothing but a final and unambiguous stare from Bea and a guarantee from Wally that he will look them up when they get settled. Their friends stay for a while, Leonard and Mel collecting glasses, trying to make amends, Beth and Anna trying to make peace. But they are helpless to build a bridge against thirty years of refined chaos.

It is Wally who finally forces them out into the freezing darkness by turning the stereo on full blast and marching on every stick of furniture big enough to plant a foot on, with Bea screaming at him from the hall, then taking a bottle of Five Star and locking herself in the upstairs bathroom. The latest prank has escalated beyond intention, beyond all reason, has become not an absurd comedy or an unbelievable story to tell at the Legion, but a weapon in the truest sense.

When their friends drive away they can see the light go on in the upstairs bathroom and Wally's shadow riding up and down the wall in the living room.

Wally is well into his seventies now, and Bea, well, she has been dead for close to ten years. She hadn't been well for a while and then one day she had a heart attack in her kitchen and died right under the spot where Wally used to do his trick with the china. He's living in a seniors' condominium, terrified that some day he'll find himself playing bridge in the games room on the main floor or helping with afternoon tea. There's a communal workshop in the basement with all kinds of tools—a tablesaw, a drill press, rotors and palm sanders, vises and bar clamps, two large workbenches—the kind of tools he never allowed himself to buy. It's a big room with a window and three banks of florescent lights, but he prefers the little space he managed to squeeze out of the laundry room in his own apartment, a room not much bigger than a closet. There's a small table wedged between the washer and dryer with the little four-inch bench vise he's had since the '50s mounted on it, a clip-on light, a piece of pegboard screwed to the wall to hold the old-fashioned handtools he's always used: flat files, hacksaws, tin snips. Some of the old crew in the Credit Unions around the province contact him once in a while to cut a special key, or rebuild a tumbler from a safe he sold them twenty or thirty years ago. If Bea was still with him, she'd go mad over the metal filings and the makeshift shelves.

He stopped making cold calls when he overheard an office girl in Moose Jaw tell the manager "some old guy" wanted to talk to him. His salesman's diplomacy is rusty, and if any of the residents happen to corner him in a conversation about the weather, he's afraid he might tell them to fuck off. It's the kind of response Bea became famous for after having a few drinks: abrupt, condemning, thoughtless. So when he leaves the building, he always scouts the hall to make sure it's safe before stepping out of the apartment. Then he hobbles to the elevator and to his car in the underground garage as fast as his reconstructed hip will allow.

He's been with Millie for a few years. Like him, she also ended up alone. They don't live together, though it's not because they think it would be sinful without being married. They see each other most days. She is a good person, a good friend, and if pressed, Wally would even say he loves her, though he wouldn't want to explain how the word "love" has come to mean something very different in his old age. He often drives her to Manitoba to visit her kids and they even take trips together in the winter to get away from the cold. Sometimes she stays over, so she keeps some clothes in the dresser and her arsenal of pills and toiletries takes up most of the space in the bathroom medicine cabinet. She's started him on a program of vitamins and mineral supplements, but that's the only concession he has agreed to. Wally says they get along better this way; that he's too old and fixed in his ways to start over again. And after all those years of spending so much time alone on the road, he just doesn't know how to have another person around all the time. With the apartment being so small, there'd be no place to hide.

The days of the week have begun to lose their form, blending into one another like subtle shades of white. He needs to defend himself against this lack of demarcation; indifference, he believes, is the first sign of giving up. So he keeps trying to have people over on Saturday nights. But their friends are disappearing into extended care units, hospitals, graves. And the ones who can still get around tire easily. On the few occasions when they get together he pulls out all the stops: garlic and beer sausage, rye bread, hot pickles, Limberger and blue cheese, whatever it takes to keep them going—an army always fights on its belly. Once, he even asked Millie to make plum pies, but they didn't turn out at all like Bea's. Bottles of Navy Rum, Five Star, Smirnoff and Seagrams are lined up on the counter, and he makes sure everyone knows it's open season.

By midnight he's primed for action, but by then the apartment is always empty, except for Millie, grumbling to herself about the pubic hair left on the toilet, the glasses and cracker crumbs on the counter, the cigarette ashes on the tiny balcony overlooking the street. She's the Tasmanian Devil in yellow rubber gloves up to her elbows, spinning from room to room as she sanitizes everything in her path.

He could tell her to leave everything alone and have another drink, but he knows what she'll say: "Someone has to clean up this mess and it obviously isn't going to be you, buster." It's the same response Bea would have, and if she were here, he would have no trouble whipping her into one of her stupendous frenzies. But Millie's resemblance to Bea is only on the surface. When Bea drank she became nasty, venomous, spitting out whatever came into her head: *Jackass. Dumkopf.* Touch a nerve and she'd twitch. There was real security back then. On those rare occasions when Millie drinks, when she allows herself to loosen up, she wants to laugh and dance. But she never gets out of control. And she's always prepared to pick up her coat and leave at the slightest tremor.

The Coldstream Guards don't march around the world anymore, and the grand finale has never been successful since Bea passed away. He tried parading around on the furniture a few times, but the neighbours complain whenever he cranks up the stereo, and Millie, though willing to call him a stupid fool, has little more than a spectator's attachment to the colonial furniture, the china and crystal in the hutch. She has her own history, her own memorabilia to dust and polish, and it's all safely stored in her own apartment. He even tried revising his marching routine, so that instead of stomping on the furniture, the goal was to make a complete circle of the room without ever touching the floor, making a point, of course, of feigning several catastrophic disasters along the way. He could easily make his way to the patio door on the couch and chair, then use the ottoman as an island to get to the recliner on the opposite side of the room. From there he would cast a doubtful look at the two end tables and the television that separated them, then raising a hand over his eyes, he would squint toward the dining area at the far end of the room as if it were a thousand miles away. Holding a Sears catalogue in his teeth, he'd edge onto the first end table on all fours, tossing the catalogue in front of the television as a stepping stone to the second end table. From there he had the option of either crawling over the centre of the colonial table or circling it by walking from chair to chair, careful to avoid hitting his head on the ceiling fan, which he always made sure was running at full before he started. He knew the plan lacked historic build-up, but he was impressed with his ability to concoct something new just for Millie.

But instead of getting mad, Millie worries that he'll fall and break his artificial hip, or kill himself flying head-first onto the coffee table. She can't stand to watch, so she either goes to bed or leaves. With her, provocation leads nowhere. He is Stanley Laurel without a Hardy. Ralph Kramden without his Alice.

When everyone is gone he puts Belafonte on the console stereo that still has the original needle in it. He turns the lights out, settles into the recliner, his good ear facing the speaker, the volume just loud enough to be heard. The record, like the stereo, is over thirty-five years old now. In places there is just as much crackling as music, and when Harry stops between songs it's hard to separate the applauding Carnegie audience from all the static that has worn its way onto the record. He knows when every skip occurs and how each one got there. He knows when the needle will get stuck in a grove, the exact moment Harry starts every line. *That is your Daddy. Oh no! My Daddy can't be ugly so.* Every word becomes a part of him for the ninety-four minutes it takes to listen to the concert from start to finish. Negro spirituals. Caribbean laments and rollicking nonsense. Spanish, Irish, Australian: a world crackling with life. He sips his drink. Closes his eyes. Fingers the loose skin under his chin.

Belafonte still sounds like a million bucks: *Wake up, wake uuuuup, darlin' Cora.* It's just the two of them now, Wally and Harry, flying through the clouds.